The Rein⟨
Camill⟨

Also by Robert Wallace

The Valentine Series

WW2 wartime spy thriller series.

Valentines Cup

Crimson Wing

Monkeypuzzle

Operation Gunfleet

One Single Ticket

A Victorian detective mystery based around the
adventures of Isambard Kingdom Brunel

The Betrayal of Jacqueline Flower

A psychological crime thriller

The Revenge of Catherine Delane

The lives of four women whose fates collide in an
explosive, unpredictable finale

Fables and Folk

A collection of urban ghost and extraordinary stories with
factual origins.

Praise for the Author

About 'One Single Ticket'

"A detective story told at a breathless pace, with a Richard Hannay type hero straight out of a John Buchan thriller, and it goes with a swing"

Professor Angus Buchanan, author of 'Brunel: The Life and Times of Isambard Kingdom Brunel

"The plot is so interesting, and the setting so well done; a delight to get a scenic picture of this special event in history."

Dr. Gabrielle Obrist, Museum of Modern Art, Zürich

About 'Valentines Cup'

'From the start, this story conveys that sense of time and place, blending actual characters from our history with fictional, but wholly plausible, characters. It does not detail the horrors of war.

A great beauty of Robert Wallace's writing is that those details aren't required. '

Rodney J. Little, Charlotte, NC

iii

About the Author

Robert Wallace was born and raised in Bristol and spent many years working in the medical field which took him to Europe, the United States, Japan, Australia and Scandinavia. It sparked a lifelong interest in travel. His work involves turning historical events into works of semi-fiction, retaining the factual background, creating fictional characters to share their lives with real people.

ROBERT WALLACE

THE REINCARNATION
OF CAMILLE BOISSIER

TradShack

The doctrine of reincarnation is neither absurd nor useless. 'It is not more surprising to be born twice than once.'

Voltaire 94-1778. Paris, France.

The Gamble

Château Boissier, Segonzac, France

"I HAVE NO WAY of winning, do I?" Gérard Boissier sounds nervous. He looks at the stack of two hundred Euros and licks his lips as if his life is suddenly about to end in a puff of smoke.

"Life is full of surprises, my friend. You never know. That is the beauty of it, surprises." Carlo Fieschi's demeanour is calm and collected. Fieschi is a man of forty; a Corsican rogue, with broad shoulders and a muscular physique gone to seed. But his eyes are those of a gambler, always calculating the odds.

Gérard is the opposite. And he's desperate to win.

The atmosphere in the wood-panelled salon is electric as the two men play chess late at night. But this is more than just a simple game for pleasure; it's a gamble; a contest of nerves and only one of them can walk away with the money.

The château in which they are sitting lies in the heart of the Grande Champagne. A French district called a cru, the French word for growth region, famous for Cognac. Château Boissier, a late eighteenth century manor, is surrounded by row after row of vines. A huge Cognac estate and Gérard and his wife Edith are the owners.

*

In a gallery above the salon, two pretty girls – twins of fifteen – clutch the wooden bannisters. Fear is in their eyes as they watch the scene below unfold. The air is thick with cigar smoke. And even they can feel the unfolding tension.

Carlo Fieschi, despite being dangerous, fascinates them because he is worldly and they are not. Goodness knows how their father knows Fieschi. Gérard is a thinly-built man with the rheumy eyes of an alcoholic. He's mid-thirties but looks older. His clothes are scruffy, face unshaven. He wears a Medic Alert Bracelet on his left wrist. The candlelight flickers, intense animosity and fierce competition are in the air. A wood fire burns in a huge open stone hearth.

The girls, blonde, blue-eyed, are fascinated as they watch the scene. It is Fieschi whose harsh tone breaks the silence:

"How much do you owe, Gérard? Your debt must be stacking up?" There is an edge to his seemingly innocent question.

Gérard fidgets nervously, slugs drink, then he notices the girls above them, staring down wide-eyed at their father's humiliation: "Jeanne! Camille! Go to bed. It's late." Fieschi pretends not to notice their presence or Gérard's discomfort. The two girls scurry off to their mother's bedroom.

Edith

Bedroom at the Château

EDITH BOISSIER, THE TWINS' mother, comes into her bedroom to find them on top of a huge old iron-framed double bed. Once she was pretty, but life has taken its toll on her delicate features: running the château, harvesting the grapes, managing the workforce, and raising her two daughters. And, living with a manic depressive with a penchant for his own produce. She wears a dressing gown, her hair wet from the bath. She's surprised to see them but smiles indulgently; they are really all she has to show from an unhappy marriage. "What's the matter?"

Camille, a few minutes younger than her sister, climbs off the bed: "Maman, the trouble is Papa and Monsieur Fieschi are being noisy, drinking. There's something wrong … with Papa. They are playing chess for money which we know Papa doesn't have." Camille acts and sounds more naïve than she really is.

"Yes. He's smoking fat cigars and the doctor told him not to," says Jeanne with authority. She looks at her sister for agreement which she receives with a brief nod. Edith glances at her watch, clearly annoyed: "They'll finish soon, it's late." Camille: "Why do they do it?"

Edith shakes her head with a 'who knows?' kind of expression.

Jeanne says imploringly: "Will you sing to us, quietly? Oh, please say you will, Maman." Edith sighs: "It's late, Genie. Besides, you're both too old for bedtime lullabies." Genie is the special nickname her mother and close family use. Jean-Genie is the reason, a favourite song by David Bowie.

"Please, Maman!" the girls say in unison. "Edith Piaf! Françoise Hardy ... even some Carole King. We know you love 'Tapestry.' We do too."

"Bien." Edith smiles and starts to hum 'You've got a friend' softly. Her tone is soothing and re-assuring: '*when you're down and troubled and you need some love and care*' ... She dims the light, gets onto the bed between them, they hug her, each vying for more attention, snuggling up to her as she now sings a Beatles melody with French lyrics. They love it: '*these are words that go together well, my Michelle*'.

*

Below, in the salon, the atmosphere is still less than cordial. Fieschi persists quietly, a hidden agenda: "How much, Gérard?"

Gérard pretends to study the chess board: "Enough, I must

5

confess." Fieschi carefully bides his time, then he looks Gérard in the eye: "I may be able to help you ... it concerns Jeanne."

Gérard is stunned "Genie? Help? How?"

"There is a part in a film for her."

"She's only fifteen, Fieschi."

Fieschi admires the glow of his Cuban cigar: "I know how old she is. The role in question calls for a fifteen- or sixteen-year-old girl." Fieschi watches his opponent carefully; he can see his greed growing over logic and responsibility. He times his coup de grâce perfectly: "And if you agree I can pay part up front. Now. Tonight." Fieschi produces a bundle of Euros and places them on the table: bait; the seeds of temptation are sown.

Gérard looks at them, chews his lip; a bead of sweat drops: "I'm-I'm not sure ... I..."

Fieschi: "You can't describe the smell of money, can you? But twenty thousand crisp Euros smells damn good. Of course, these are mainly twenties and a few tens. Everyone is suspicious of fifties after that counterfeit mob got caught near Criteuil-la-Magdeleine awhile back. An underground printing press, remember? Even made the nationals!"

"Yes." He rarely sees a fifty unless Edith has one.

Gérard's hand automatically moves towards the money, but Fieschi is quicker and snaps the tempting bundle away: "Wait. You'll want to know more about the role? Yes? What part she

6

might be able to play? And maybe sing?"

Gérard nods. Fieschi studies his adversary with relish; a predator: "And this will more than solve your problems, Gérard. Huh?"

Gérard's voice sounds nervous: "What would she have to do?"

Fieschi puffs on his cigar and blows smoke away dismissively: "Oh! Act. We can teach her. She has the perfect face." He doesn't say 'and body too', but it is all he can think about. God, there are brides younger than her in some cultures. He smiles and mentally justifies his barter. Yes, she has the perfect everything. Fieschi removes his hand from the bundle of cash, lightens his tone and continues his pitch persuasively: "Yes, we have people – experienced women – who can coach her. Think about Vanessa Paradis. By the time she reached 18, she was awarded France's highest honours as both a singer and an actress with the Prix Romy Schneider and the César Award for most promising actress." He pauses for effect. "Yes, quite an achievement ... I can see Jeanne being much the same."

"What about Camille?"

"I think we both realise Jeanne would be better suited to the eye of the camera. And she's a little more, what, mature? Plus, her voice is more gracious." He pauses again. "That's no offence to Camille. She is beautiful too. They are twins, for God's sake!" He laughs boisterously at his own joke.

Gérard is hesitant.

7

"Well? What do you think?"

Indecision is written all over Gérard's face. And yet ... and yet.

"It's all perfectly legitimate. Someone like Charlotte Aubier will handle her to start off with; yes, I can arrange that, I'm certain. A voice coach will help improve her technique and there are acting schools. Everything she needs ..."

Gérard looks up, hearing a female name as a coach. Maybe it will be ok after all. Maybe I am just being a little over-cautious.

Fieschi pours him another slug of Cognac: "But you must sign an agreement, a contract, because of her age ... Yes, I think that will make sense, Gérard. For your peace of mind." But Gérard, despite everything, is wary: "A contract?"

Fieschi loads his response with nonchalance: "Yes, I know it's a nuisance." He pauses with a little snigger... "A minor technicality for the film company. You know how it is..." Gérard shakes his head: no, he doesn't know how it is. He tends Cognac vines and looks after the soil. He just happens to have a beautiful, stunning daughter. Two in fact. And there is not a lot he can do about it.

"Did you hear what I was saying, Gérard?" The Corsican loads on the charm. "Thought I'd lost you for a moment ..."

"No."

A smile of reassurance, Fieschi continues convincingly: "...Nothing to do with me. A legal requirement. I'll make her a star, Gérard. She is naturally talented. Think of it as an investment."

8

"I, I don't know." His hesitancy is clear.

Fieschi waits because this bit is tricky: "Does Edith know the mess you're in?"

"Leave her out of this." Gérard says sharply and glances into the cold eyes of his adversary.

"Oh. I see."

Fieschi cunningly places some more Euros on the table. Gérard stares at them, seeing freedom very close to him now.

Fieschi takes out a contract and an expensive old fountain pen: "And when she is famous, we'll all be very – what's the word – happy? No, proud."

Fieschi slides the contract across to Gérard and unscrews the pen.

"Won't I need a lawyer? A witness?"

Fieschi now knows the bait has been taken, just a nibble and needs to be reeled in. He stands, walks to the logs burning in the open stone hearth, and relights his cigar with a taper. His back is turned, and he can't help smirking:

"You make a valid point, Gérard. But it will save you money if I was your witness. And we already have a lawyer – Serge Antonelli – reliable and one of mine, so to speak." Gérard touches the money, indecision in his face. And hope. A deadly balance. Suddenly Fieschi swings around, Gérard snaps his hand away, too late, caught. But timing is part of the Machiavellian process.

9

Fieschi looks benevolent: "Well, my friend?"

"I am not your friend, Fieschi. We both know that."

Fieschi pretends to look crestfallen: "Oh! And I do enjoy our games of chess, Gérard. I thought you did too." He stops, tempted to ask - well, my friend? - again, but knows not to. Gérard stares up at the landing where his daughters had been watching – no sign of them now. Gérard knows he has no choice. And so does Fieschi. The tension in the salon is unbearable.

"Alright."

"The right decision, Gérard."

Gérard scans the contract, his eyes bleary with booze and smoke. He signs it with Fieschi's proffered fountain pen. Fieschi watches very carefully, then picks the contract up and waves it around to dry. Folds it, pockets it. "Good." He puts on his jacket, downs his drink.

Gérard glances up at him, surprised: "We haven't finished the game yet ... I think we digressed somewhat." A forced snigger that doesn't work.

Fieschi smiles: "I think we have ... I concede." Fieschi pats him on the shoulder, pushes the twenty thousand Euros across the chessboard towards him, but accidentally forgets his fountain pen. "Yes, you won this evening in many ways."

Gérard: "What will I tell Edith?"

"The truth, of course, Gérard. Jeanne will be a star. Tell her you persuaded me ... imagine, the girl from Segonzac mingling in Parisian showbiz circles. Ah, I can see it." Fieschi leaves without another word.

Gérard sits alone, stares at the money. He's just sold his daughter. He swigs from the bottle, flicks through the notes. The salon door opens suddenly; Edith comes in and waves her hands to disperse the tendrils of cigar smoke hanging in the room. She looks at the distraught Gérard and sees the stack of Euros and the unfinished game of chess. Several bank notes float to the floor, adding to the mysterious scene she finds. She picks one up, regards it and comes closer to Gérard.

"What's this?"

"I won, what do you think?"

Edith looks deeply suspicious, eyes him carefully: "That will be a first." She moves to the table, picks up Fieschi's elegant fountain pen. "What have you done, Gérard?"

He tries to protect his cash, but she persists: "What?"

Gérard stands unsteadily, can't look her in the eye. A few more bank notes take flight as he finds one word: "Nothing."

Her tone kicks up a notch; she knows he's lying: "What? I sense trouble." Gérard summons the words suggested by Fieschi earlier: "Well, actually, I managed to persuade Carlo ..." a judicious use of his first name ... "to have Jeanne star – appear - in one of his movies."

11

His words take her breath away: "You did what?"

"At first, he didn't agree, but I talked him round. He just couldn't see it at first as I could. You know, the girl from Segonzac mingling with Parisian society ..." his words sound false and she can hear his deceitfulness. She's used to it.

"Oh really. You talked him around? What's the film about?" Edith couldn't be more suspicious.

Gérard persists: "He paid an upfront fee. Look, it will get us out of trouble." Edith: "Us?" She points Fieschi's pen at Gérard. "Have you signed something without having the common decency to ... to ask me? I am your wife, Gérard." But lying is not his forte: "Just a contract."

Common sense is hers: "Just a contract? And did you ask Genie?" "There is no need. No, I am her father."

"And that gives you the right to plan her life?" Edith is shouting with disbelief at his arrogance and stupidity.

"She's my daughter ...," he persists on a hiding to nothing.

"No! You fool! She's our daughter. And what about Camille? Have you considered her feelings? They are very close."

"Fieschi says Jeanne will look good on camera." He doesn't realise he used the surname now, not Carlo as before. But Edith picks up immediately.

"Oh, Fieschi says! They're twins for God's sake. They look the same. Sometimes I wonder about you, Gérard. I really do. What goes on in that addled brain of yours. D'you think I'm completely stupid?"

"No. But Fieschi thinks ..."

She cuts in, livid. Edith is boiling: "Fieschi's obsessed with Genie. I've seen him looking at her. He's a sick man. A Corsican version of Harvey Weinstein."

"No."

"Yes! He craves power over women, the casting couch. I've seen it in his eyes." "That's not ..."

Suddenly Edith yells: "You sold your daughter."

"No."

"Yes."

Gérard is near tears: "I would never do that, Edith. Never."

Edith slams the fountain pen back down so hard it leaks ink, spreading like a black blood stain across the wooden table. They both silently watch it. "You just did. You sold her to get yourself out of the shit. That's the truth. You sold your own flesh and blood ... one of our precious girls." Edith breaks down. "Our Angels."

He picks up the bottle, puts it to his lips. Just as he does, she smacks it out of his hand in sheer anger. It smashes into the red-hot embers in the open stone hearth and the Cognac ignites into flames. Edith screams out at him: "How could you be so selfish?" She fails to notice the escalating fire and growing heat; she is so incensed by him. Suddenly Gérard cuffs her across the face with

13

the back of his hand. The blow has such power and impact that it sends her flying across to the open hearth. Her head cracks on the stone grate. She goes straight down.

The flames from the hearth are spreading to the wood panelling surrounding it and creeping towards the floorboards, like an indoor bushfire. Edith lies there motionless, her eyes closed, blood pumping from a head wound. In the flickering light it looks as if it's spreading in the shape of a black eagle. Gérard stands a moment, then collapses to his knees in regret, crying. He's desperately shocked and can't believe what he's done. He crawls along on his hands and knees towards Edith's inert body and shakes her arm for a response. Then, finding nothing, he breaks down completely.

He grabs another bottle of Cognac and smashes it into another section of wood wall panelling. The whole salon ignites into a ball of flames with a whoosh. He's out of control as he watches the flames licking the walls and heading for the ceiling. Suddenly the two girls come charging down the stairs, screaming. Then they see their dead mother and barge Gérard out of their way. Her dressing gown is starting to smoulder. Jeanne and Camille are frantic and don't know what to do. At that precise moment, there is a loud thumping on the front door. It flies open. Fieschi is there. He quickly takes it all in, but he's not surprised at what he sees, given the state Gérard was in earlier. But how could the situation have escalated to this carnage? And so quickly.

Fieschi shouts: "My God! No!" He runs over to Edith, gathers her up in his arms and yells at the girls: "Get out of here, you two! Now! Go!"

Escape

THE GIRLS ARE HESITANT at first; frozen with fear and frightened to leave. Gérard runs towards the salon doorway but falls to the floor in drunken panic. Fieschi takes Edith outside and lays her gently down on the grass in the secluded garden. He brushes strands of hair from her face and tries to rouse her. He looks over his shoulder at the girls and yells out at them: "Get out of there. It's dangerous. Can't you ..." he doesn't finish the sentence. He charges back into the house and scoops Jeanne off her feet and runs out with her, lays her down near to her dead mother. Jeanne is shaking with emotion, overwhelmed with the situation ... Fieschi runs back in, and grabs Camille. Seconds elapse. He watches the fire rage in the wooden salon and charges back out again with Camille.

Outside, Jeanne is cradling her mother's head in her lap, stroking her hair, her face. Tears stream down her cheeks: "Maman is dead, Camille. I think Papa must have killed her. Look at her head ..." Jeanne's hand is covered in her mother's blood. Edith's head wound looks shocking from her collision with the open stone hearth and Jeanne can't take her eyes off it.

Fieschi runs over to the tragic scene and anxiously feels for Edith's pulse – both neck – and wrist. He can't find anything and shakes his head sorrowfully at the girls. Next, he attempts to resuscitate her: CPR – chest compressions, combined with mouth to mouth. Finally, after more than five minutes of trying, he collapses across Edith's body, breathless with exertion. "It's useless girls, she's gone. I am so sorry." He looks up at the two broken hearted faces. "At least you tried, Monsieur," one of them says.

He sits himself up: "Yes."

Behind them Gérard is screaming. Suddenly, Camille runs back towards the doorway wild with anger. Gérard's foot appears trapped in the fractured burning floorboards between the salon and hallway. He screams: "Please get me out of here. Please – please help me."

Camille is running towards him in blind desperation. She grabs hold of Gérard's sleeve. Fieschi and Jeanne can't see if she is pulling or pushing. He falls back into the fire; the bracelet comes off his wrist and vanishes. Camille is confused, disorientated in the smoke and heat. Fieschi takes out a Canon IXUS compact camera and rapidly takes pictures. Using the Optical Zoom, he can capture exactly the images he wants. Altering the angle from portrait to landscape adds more variation. Jeanne is puzzled: what's he doing? And why? She looks at him for an explanation.

"Oh, your parents' insurers will need evidence. Assessors are picky, believe me." The throwaway gesture adds credence to his statement. Supposedly.

But Jeanne is suspicious: it's a fire – what more evidence do they need? From the burning floorboards below her, Gérard suddenly grabs hold of Camille's ankle to save himself and she falls onto her side, down onto the burning floorboards. Seconds pass and then the flaming wooden floor fragments, splitting open and swallowing Gérard completely. He drops into the bowels of the building, his screams echoing as his body collides against the cellar walls. Finally, it hits the stone floor with a resounding thump. Released from his grip, Camille struggles up onto her hands and knees and finally stands. She's lost and disorientated in the smoke, staring down at the hole which had taken her father. Her clothes are badly singed, and the side of her face is already burned and blistering from the cruel flames.

Fieschi tells Jeanne to stay where she is and sprints back towards the entrance to the château where Camille is standing paralyzed with shock.

"Wait there, Camille," he yells, "I must go back in and look for my mobile to call for help. I left it on the table and I ..." He never finishes the sentence, too desperate.

*

Inside the château's smoke-filled salon, Fieschi runs back to the table where Gérard and he had been playing chess, his hand over his mouth, fighting the noxious fumes. Fieschi hastily gathers up the twenty thousand Euros from the chessboard, desperately stuffing the notes into every available pocket. He grabs his precious antique fountain pen, silently cursing himself for leaving it there. There is no phone to retrieve; it's been in his pocket all the time.

A quick look around to confirm there is nothing left to incriminate him. He taps his jacket pocket with a wry smile. The Contract is safe and that's all that matters. He runs back out towards the salon door where Camille is still standing beside the hole which swallowed her father. He steps around it and helps her away to safety, ignoring the state of her face and clothes. And then, in that moment of supposed protection from harm, he delivers the bombshell: "You pushed him, Camille. You killed your father." She screams: "No ... I was trying to save him ... wasn't I?"

"No. He killed your mother, Camille. I don't blame you."

She sobs: "No. No. No. Please?"

"Yes, Camille. I saw you. And I have the proof to destroy your life. Remember that." His cruel words dumfound her. She sobs again in utter disbelief as he pulls her away from the scene to join her sister. She doesn't mention the pain she is suffering.

Rescue

THEY TURN MOMENTARILY TO see a mighty flaming roof beam drop down and block the doorway to the château completely. The noise is tremendous. Fieschi takes Camille by the arm, pretending to escort her politely back to where Jeanne and her mother are. To all intents and purposes, he appears to be a Good Samaritan. There is no sign on his face of the horrendous threat he'd just made to an injured girl of fifteen. A girl who'd just lost both her parents and her home.

They find Jeanne and their late mother lying beside the château in the secluded garden. The shadows and light dance around on the grass like evil spirits.

"Here we are, Camille. Come and sit with your sister. I have called the emergency services." He taps his pocket and explains to Jeanne what he had done: "Whoa! I had to run back in to get my mobile ... I'd left it on the chess table ... stupid me ... my brain. I must be getting old." He smiles at the two girls; they will remember that he'd risked his life, running through flames to get the phone to make the call to save them. There is no mention of the twenty thousand Euros he'd jammed into his pockets, or the distinctive fountain pen he'd retrieved. The Contract signed by Gérard is a secret, for the moment, at least.

The look of benevolence on his face does not betray the evil in his heart. Jeanne and Camille look at him; for a moment he feels as if they are trying to read his mind; but luckily, they can't. His face suddenly breaks into an expression of joyous emotion: "Ah! Listen, girls! Can you hear the sirens? I can! Thank God the emergency services are on their way here to help us."

"Too late to help our parents though, monsieur." Jeanne's tone is acerbic; she cannot know Fieschi threatened Camille. But she senses something is not entirely right and turns to her sister. "Isn't that right, Camille?"

But Camille says nothing, still too choked to speak. And in desperate pain. Fieschi looks at Jeanne and narrows his eyes: "Yes, but lucky you had me, or you'd both be dead. Just remember that. Stay here." He stands and walks toward the approaching vehicles.

Jeanne rolls her eyes in defiance, a trait that will define her personality forever. Camille is the opposite: resolute, but calm. Even after what she has been through tonight. Camille takes Jeanne's hand: "I need to tell you something."

"I know you do."

21

*

Moments later, a car pulls up and a plain clothes policeman jumps out. Inspector Gaston Leclerc is a seen-it-all policeman of the Nouvelle-Aquitaine region. Despite his experience he is shocked at what he sees. The Pompiers – firefighters – have just arrived at the scene and are already attending the blaze with hoses. Leclerc – always known as Gaston - hurries over to where Fieschi, Jeanne and Camille are sitting on the grass with Edith's body a short distance away from them. Fieschi has respectfully covered her with his raincoat. But it is still disturbing for Gaston to see the girls with their dead mother. And a stranger. Gaston shows them his ID: "Leclerc. Cognac Commissariat de Police. Is anyone else in the building?"

"No," says Fieschi. "We're the survivors."

He sighs: "I need to know what happened." His eyes scan the burning Château Boissier. Jeanne, coldly: "Mr. Fieschi saved our lives."

Gaston looks at Edith's inert body and then at Fieschi, who nods in acknowledgement. "But not our mother's...." Jeanne is interrupted by the arrival of a paramedic at the scene in an ambulance. She gets out, comes over and sees Camille's face.

Gaston: "Hello. Glad you're here."

"I'm Margot, one of the paramedics." She squats down so she is on the same level as Fieschi and the girls. "Tell me what happened." Jeanne gives her a brief synopsis; simultaneously

22

Margot opens her bag and starts to cool Camille's burnt face and shoulder with a cold compress and, after ten minutes, applies non-stick sterile dressing. Fieschi watches without a word.

"Right," says Margot decisively, gently taping the dressing. "That will do for the time being. Hold that dressing against your face. We need to get you both to hospital. Cognac is nearest." She turns to Jeanne. "These burns need to be looked at by a doctor and properly dressed, alright?"

Camille says nothing.

Jeanne and Fieschi both nod. Margot continues, addressing both girls: "Plus you will both be suffering from smoke inhalation. And dehydration. Do you need to call anyone? ... You can use my phone." She looks at the two distraught faces, already knowing the answer. But it is her duty to ask them anyway.

Jeanne shakes her head sadly: "There is no one now." Margot instinctively takes the girls' hands, her face full of compassion. They are immediately taken with her warmth and understanding of the delicate situation.

"We should go ... are you both alright to walk?" Jeanne and Camille nod and stand; and, as they do so, Margot turns to Fieschi: "You look ok, sir. But you need to see a doctor all the same. Alright? And that means soonest." Her assertion is polite.

Fieschi agrees as she leads the two girls to the open ambulance. Another paramedic is there ready to cover their shoulders with blankets.

23

"Thank you, Margot," Gaston calls out to her. "I'll call the hospital in the morning for an update." Margot raises her arm in a gesture of agreement. "She's a fine girl, that Margot. Known her since she was a child." He surveys the smouldering building and turns to Fieschi: "You're all lucky to be alive from what I can see. This is tragic."

Another ambulance arrives and two paramedics discreetly lift Edith's body onto a stretcher. They remove the raincoat – hand it to Fieschi - and replace it with blanket. Gaston turns his attention back to Fieschi as they take Edith away.

He conceals his involvement in the tragedy: "Yes, it was lucky I came back. I can't imagine what happened here tonight, officer."

Gaston looks far from happy: "You'll need to answer some questions, Mr. ..." "I am Carlo Fieschi ... the film producer. I'm sure you've seen many of my ..." "Perhaps later, sir. Lots to do. But please stay on site." Gaston watches the embers of the château as the ambulance carrying Camille and Jeanne is driven away to hospital. He asks Fieschi for some details; and he is almost over-cooperative.

Gaston takes out his phone: "Sir, Leclerc. At Château Boissier, near Segonzac. Two dead; Gérard and Edith Boissier. Their daughters – Jeanne and Camille – are on their way to Cognac A&E with Margot Gauthier, the paramedic. One of the girls, I don't know which, has some nasty burns to her face ... yes ... one witness is here on site ... alright, sir. I'll bring him in later, but Margot reckons he needs to be checked over by a medic too ... yes, he can make a statement at the station ... indeed, yes ... good night, sir. Sorry to have disturbed you so late, but I knew you'd want an update."

Gaston turns to Fieschi: "I'm sure you got the gist of that?"

Fieschi nods: "But I don't need a doctor. I'm fine."

Gaston grins: "If Margot Gauthier says you need to see a doctor ... you do. Trust me."

Café

THE FOLLOWING MORNING, Jeanne and Fieschi are sitting together at a table in the café. He clutches her hand, playing the part of the overindulgent guardian. Dr Dominique Brousse, a doctor in her thirties enters the café, looks around, sees Fieschi and Jeanne and comes over. She's casually dressed in a tweed skirt and blouse, her stethoscope around her neck. Clipped to her skirt is a medical on-call beeper; she's carrying hospital notes, printed scans and her mobile. She joins them at their table, removes her glasses and exudes an air of compassion and authority. The lengthy conversation she'd had with Gaston earlier has given her an overview of what happened at the château the previous evening. His view, at least.

"Jeanne, good morning. My name is Dominique Brousse, one of the doctors here." Fieschi and Jeanne nod politely.

26

"I thought here would make more sense than the ward. Plus the waiting room is out of action with decorators. I hope that's alright?"

"Can I get you a coffee?" asks Fieschi, with a nod.

"No, let's get on. Thank you anyway."

Dominique acknowledges Fieschi but establishes sympathetic eye contact with Jeanne and addresses her directly. "I see from your notes that you are fifteen years old. Is it alright for me to speak freely in front of this gentleman? Is he a family friend or relative? It is my duty to ask you this."

Jeanne gives a faint smile: "It's alright for you to speak freely, yes." Dominique breathes a sigh of relief: "Sorry to appear – sound – so formal, but patient confidentiality is paramount. Especially concerning a minor. Apologies Mr ..." Fieschi says: "No problem. Fieschi."

Dominique resumes: "Last night we admitted into Emergency ..." But Jeanne interrupts her: "How's my sister? Will she be – will she be – alright?" Dominique is frank: "Yes, she will. She is stable now, but she will have to remain in the Intensive Care Unit for several days. The last thing she needs is an infection."

"Thank you, doctor."

Dominique consults her notes: "Camille is on an I.V. drip. Do you know what that is?"

"I have seen them on TV, yes."

"The drip is to administer intravenous drugs and fluids to help her recover fully. Antibiotics to prevent the infection we spoke about, morphine for pain relief and we are sedating her because of the trauma. She's very upset ... there is no mirror in the ICU bathroom, not that she needs to get there at the moment ... do you see what I mean, Jeanne? What I am saying?"

Jeanne understands exactly: "When can I see her?"

Dominique nods, impressed at Jeanne's maturity: "Later this morning, but don't forget, she will be sleepy from the medication. And you will have to wear a special mask and gown."

"Yes, because of germs."

"Yes, bacteria; but you are correct, germs." She pauses. "Now I know this is very difficult for you, Jeanne, but please try not to worry too much. Camille is in very safe hands and she will recover. We have learned a great deal about burns over the years."

"Thank you, doctor," Jeanne says again.

Dominique takes her hand: "Is there any support you need? Anyone the hospital can contact? Relatives?"

Dominique scrutinises Fieschi and Jeanne carefully for a reaction.

But it is Fieschi who answers: "No thank you, Dr. Brousse. Her aunt Bénédicte is far too old for such responsibility. You've been very kind but I can take care of her now." Dominique's on-call beeper buzzes and she unclips it from her skirt to look at the message: "I'm needed. A&E. Now, Jeanne, you are sure this is alright? Mr Fieschi can look after you?"

"Yes, doctor."

"I'll let social services know. I must run. Here is a card with my name and mobile number. Or you can call the hospital switchboard and they can beep me. Anytime, alright?"

"Thank you."

Dominique looks at her watch: "Camille is in ICU on the second floor. Ask the nurse for bay 12. But leave it an hour, alright? I may see you later." With that she stands, gathers her belongings from the table and leaves. Fieschi had gone to the counter of the café to get himself a coffee and Jeanne a soft drink.

He returns to the table. Fieschi moves in closer and lowers his voice. Jeanne is immediately concerned by the look on his face.

"Not so bad then, eh?"

Jeanne says nothing because everything is bad. And suspicious.

Fieschi continues: "Now, we have a little problem here because I saw Camille push your father into the fire, so did you."

She is shocked and confused: "I, I don't know what I saw." How can he be so cruel?

"No? But I did. And here is the evidence."

He takes out his Canon compact camera and flicks though six crucial images on the screen: Gérard trapped in the doorway at the château; Camille is there ... but what is she doing? Pulling or

29

pushing her father? Jeanne shakes her head in doubt: these pictures have nothing to do with her late parents' insurers; or the assessors. This is blackmail. But for what? What does he want from her? From them? She shivers with rising terror.

Fieschi's tone is one of avuncular concern, as he twists the truth. Finally, the image of Gérard dropping down through the burning wooden floorboards to the cellar below. Fieschi continues: "But you see, I think I understand. Gérard must have lost his mind. I can't think why. Can you?"

Jeanne knows he is trying to trick her but plays along. It is her only choice: "Because he ... killed our mother."

"Yes, exactly. And that's why Camille pushed him into the fire. He burned alive." Jeanne is sobbing with emotion.

Fieschi leans forward: "I will make sure that no one discovers the truth of what Camille did. It will be our secret, but you must do exactly as I say. Understand?" Jeanne is silent, looks down. The trap is set. He waits.

"I said, do you understand, Jeanne?"

A vague nod, she blinks tears as he continues: "If the authorities hear ... it will mean prison ... solitary confinement ... no visitors ... or an institution, even worse. What goes on in those places ..." He shudders theatrically. "I've heard awful things ... physical and mental abuse ... awful."

Jeanne's eyes widen at the full impact of Fieschi's words. She nods reluctantly, lips trembling.

Fieschi is full of compassion: "But that will not happen. I will protect you both. You will come and live with me. I will deal with the château and manage your financial affairs; you are too young to understand such things. I bet you don't even have a bank account, do you? Either of you?"

"No."

"I thought not. I have lawyers and experts who can protect your finances and inheritance with trust funds. Talk to the tax authorities so you are not liable. Do you understand?" "Not really ... what's a trust fund?"

He laughs in an avuncular manner: "No matter. As I said, leave it all with me. Think of me as your Uncle Carlo."

"Why are you helping us, Mr. Fieschi? And how will we ever repay you for your kindness?" Her question implies she has been completely taken in by his lies. Fieschi takes her hand and looks her in the eye: "Don't concern yourself now. Your father and I were great friends. Best friends ... even though he beat me at chess!" Jeanne laughs: "Alright then, if you say so."

"Good, good, good, my dear." Fieschi rubs his hands together, satisfied: "Now, what did Dominique say? ICU, second floor? Ask the nurse for bay 12? Let's go and see your sister soon."

Jeanne says nothing; her mind is in such a whirl. But one thing is for sure: she doesn't trust Fieschi, and she must be on her guard all the time. Suddenly she remembers the conversation she and Camille had overheard in the gallery above the salon that night.

31

The night of the fire: her father and Fieschi were not best friends. Far from it.

Fieschi's eyes flash angrily: "I said, let's go and see your sister. Now, come on. I haven't got all day."

Funeral

Rue De L'Eglise,
Lignières-Sonneville, Poitou-Charente

A FEW WEEKS LATER, outside the village church, a dozen or so mourners gather. Fieschi, Jeanne and Camille stand behind the funeral cortege, their backs turned. He's holding their hands, walking slowly. The sombre scene is interrupted only by the sound of distant organ music. A solitary mourner approaches Bénédicte, an elderly lady dressed in black:

"Bénédicte, your nieces are lucky, despite everything that's happened to them. Losing their parents like that."

Bénédicte is wary of the whole situation, but placates her neighbour nonetheless: "Oh, I'm too old to be their guardian. And besides, I wasn't asked. It seems Mr. Carlo Fieschi has assumed that role ..." She lowers her voice and says to herself: a Corsican gangster is what I've heard and I don't trust him one bit. He's shifty.

"Oh, that's too bad, Bénédicte. Fancy not even being asked. I'd be offended."

Auction

Sotheby's, New Bond Street, London

MALCOLM DILLISTONE IS A LEGEND, easily the most successful auctioneer in London. His suit as well-cut, his shirt tailor-made and his voice distinctive. Deep, mellifluous, and persuasive. Beside the podium at which he is standing, is a table. The object upon it is the centre of the auction room's attention.

A single bottle of Massougnes Cognac, 1802.

Malcolm regards two hundred potential bidders through pince-nez; his blue eyes scan the expectant faces. It's all about timing and a little humour.

"Coming up next is LOT 222 ... the second lot from the same seller as the Armagnac. I believe this bottle may have originated in France ..." A titter of nervous laughter ... "An 1802 Massougnes Cognac ... incredibly rare, from the Napoleonic era ... Let's start the bidding at £200,000 ... anyone out there feeling adventurous?"

Another ripple of amusement; but the air is charged with

energy.

"This precious liquid is presented in a 3.41-litre demijohn style bottle, which is in great condition after more than 200 years ... thank you, sir ... two-hundred thousand pounds, paddle 4 ..." Malcolm scribbles his obligatory note.

Curious heads turn to the back to see who has already committed to such a huge amount of money.

"May we say £210,000 ... anybody? ... I am told the Massougnes estate closed in 1874, after phylloxera ate its way through vines all over Europe a few years prior ... two hundred and ten thousand I am bid ... thank you, sir ... paddle 9 at the front ... jolly good." More craning of necks. More whispers. More intrigue.

"Ah," says Malcolm, "two hundred and twenty thousand on the telephone ... thank you Nancy. Anyone in the room? I can go to £225,000 if it will help. A tiny increment." Whispers into mobile phones, hushed voices.

"Massougnes produced historically famous pre-phylloxera Cognacs." Malcolm emphasizes the words for effect. "I understand we have dated their records back to 1730, making them the oldest firm of growers in the world ... thank you, sir, two-hundred and thirty-five thousand pounds I am bid by paddle 9 at the front ..."

The atmosphere is now palpable.

"Those pesky little insects – native to North America – have a lot to answer for ... making this bottle not only a piece of Cognac history, but world history ... Napoleon Bonaparte may have enjoyed a tipple of this ... Nancy, thank you ... two hundred and forty thousand pounds on the telephone ... we're getting close."

'This must be a record,' someone says. 'Imagine!'

Malcolm becomes serious: "£250, 000 I am now bid. I am selling this Cognac. Make no mistake. Anyone? Thank you, sir. For the last time ... two hundred and fifty thousand ... are we all done?" His eyes glide over the sea of faces in front of him. The gavel goes down with a bang: "Sold to ... can I see your paddle again, sir, thank you." He makes a note, but he won't forget either the number or the firm's commission. "Thank you. Right, moving on, LOT 223 ... Château Lafite Rothschild 1869 ..." A gloved porter removes the Cognac with the greatest care as another arrives with the next bottle. At the back of the room, the seller, Louis Doupeux takes out his mobile: "Bénédicte it's me. I've sold 1,000 bottles of the 1875 Armagnac and the 1802 Massougnes. I can now retire to La Rochelle ... oh, the other bottle, the 1805. You can have that as a parting gift ... I'm sorry I let you down, Bénédicte. I'll make it up to you one day, I promise."

Fieschi

Confiserie Boissier,
40 Rue du Poitou, 75003, Paris

SOME YEARS AFTER THE FUNERAL in Lignières-Sonneville,
Fieschi buys an ailing confiserie – confectioners - in Paris for
Camille; she's just over eighteen. He's discovered she has a natural
aptitude for business which the current owners clearly didn't. Mrs.
Palledri, his housekeeper, has been teaching her the rudiments of
cooking; confectionery proves to be her forte. Fieschi has two
motives: he wants to get Camille out of his apartment on Rue
Guénégaud and into her own accommodation. The confiserie will
be an ideal distraction for her. His second motive is that he's
grooming Jeanne for his own selfish purpose; her career in acting
is only a part of that ambition.

One late winter's afternoon Fieschi comes into the confiserie
unexpectedly. His chauffeur-driven limo is parked illegally outside
the shop. Fieschi has a Kashmiri coat draped over his shoulders,

trying to look cool, but it just doesn't work. He's far too short and dumpy, and she's longing for it to slide off him and into a puddle of dirty rainwater. "Hello, Camille," he says brightly.

Her heart sinks: "Hello, Fieschi. She can never bring herself to call him Carlo and certainly not Uncle; even though he's acted as guardian for her and her sister since the fire. "How's trade?" He gazes into the chiller cabinets at the selection of goodies on sale: nougat, caramel au beurre salé and petits fours. There are choux pastry cases filled with custard, cream and topped with chocolate. "Give me one of those," he points with a stubby finger, leaving a greasy smear on the pristine glass.

"It's called Religieuse ... as I'm sure you know ... coming up." She lifts it out using special pastry tongs and places it carefully onto a cardboard plate and hands it across the counter to him.

"Thanks, Camille." He greedily devours the whole thing, more or less in one go. Residues of chocolate and cream drip down his chin. He chomps noisily, making appreciative sounds as he eats: "Delicious."

Camille winces with disgust, praying no other customers come in to witness such appalling manners: "What do you want, Fieschi?"

His tongue darts out of his mouth and brushes his lips: "Just keeping an eye on my investment, that's all. And I was hungry, needed a sugar rush."

"You don't need to. I'm fine." She looks away from him. "It

39

almost runs itself." Fieschi glances out through the shop window: a parking attendant is giving his chauffeur a telling off. "I have to go." He wipes his mouth with a handkerchief and looks around the confiserie:

"Never forget who owns this shop, Camille." He walks out without another word, leaving a poisonous atmosphere hanging in the air.

Camille suddenly sobs, a gasp she cannot control: I'll never forget who owns both of us.

Michel

Château Boissier, Segonzac, France

THE MAN IS CANADIAN. He's about thirty; a quirky, off-beat character from Quebec. He's tall and rugged, dressed in an old Ben Sherman shirt and Levi jeans. He looks like a cowboy. Or a truck driver. But he's neither. He's very interested in this particular property: a burned out eighteenth century château in the heart of the Grande Champagne. He's holding an estate agent's portfolio and a mobile. He photographs different aspects of the château and its commanding views of the neglected rows of vines. Ugni Blanc and Colombard grapes with the high acidity needed to meet the criteria of the Charentais distillation process. He'd done his homework and needed to be thorough if he was going to achieve what he intended. He opens his mobile and punches numbers: "Monsieur Antonelli, s'il vous plaît ... ah yes ... please tell him it's Michel Bouchard. I'm at Château Boissier now. And I have a few questions. OK, I'll call him back if he's busy. Thanks."

Memorial

Château Boissier, Secluded Garden

THE GIRL IS FRENCH. She's in her early twenties, fair-haired, oval-shaped face and blue eyes. She wears a summer dress and moves around the secluded garden with grace and economy. There are three memorial stones set amongst the flowers and grass. It looks and feels tranquil. This is the place where her mother Edith had been laid to rest the night of the fire. She remembers the kindness of Margot Gauthier – the paramedic who attended them – and took them to Cognac hospital. And Gaston Leclerc. She squats down with a garland of fresh flowers and puts them on the exact spot where her dead mother lay, her mind a whirl of memories.

She's beautiful, sad, absorbed. Carved into the third stone is the memorial to her mother, where she stays for twenty minutes. Then she stands and walks towards the rear of the château to a ramshackle collection of old barns and Cognac chais – sheds –

where producers store Cognac in casks. Discarded agricultural vehicles and a rusty old tractor lie dormant and neglected. Slowly she opens a large wooden door with her outstretched right hand and she's inside amongst a clutter of old Cognac barrels and farm machinery. It's semi-dark, and silent. Bright shafts of sunlight shine through the broken roof. They shimmer and dance before her, illuminating tiny dust particles. Her breaths are audible.

Just ahead of her on a flat stone wall are two small child handprints of white paint: a left and a right. She places her right hand over the right print, covers the image completely, then she closes her eyes tightly.

Immediately she is transported back in time to the same place five years earlier. She can feel herself crying and there is nothing she can do about it. The memory is vivid: two young blonde twin girls watching their father Gérard at work. An old door is suspended across two barrels to form a makeshift work bench. On it are brushes, rags, spirit and a roller in a shallow tray of white paint. Gérard smiles at his two young angels. He takes Camille's left hand and carefully places her palm, flat down into the paint tray. He presses her hand against the wall, removes it slowly and leaves a very distinct white handprint. Camille beams with undisguised naïve pleasure.

Gérard's words are clear in the girl's mind: There! For posterity.

He does the same with Jeanne's right hand, next to her sister's and then cleans their hands very meticulously with spirit-soaked rags. The twins are giggling at their father's antics. The girl hears her own young voice: But what's that for, Papa? Gérard's words again: 'For future generations, my two angels'.

She opens her eyes; her hand still rests on her print. The tears stream down her face, she's shaking with emotion. Her breaths are deep. She controls them, taking in air. Her father's words echo in her mind. She snaps her hand away, looks down at her palm, she's transfixed. For a split second, it looks wet with fresh white paint.

In that moment she knows her father has been with her: is it a premonition of something out of her control? Suddenly, she turns and runs back out into the daylight, sobbing. The large old wooden door clunks shut behind her.

Encounter

Château Boissier, Secluded Garden

MICHEL BOUCHARD IS CALLING the same man back.

"Monsieur Antonelli? It's Michel Bouchard. Yes, I'm back on site again. Is there electricity connected to the château? ... OK ... What about water? ... I'd like to know a little of the history ... what? ... You're breaking up. I'll call you later."

Michel walks around, taking a few last shots before he leaves.

*

The girl is now sitting behind the wheel of a battered old Citroën 2CV. She is tearful and pre-occupied. She clunks the awkward shift into reverse. She doesn't look behind her.

CRASH!

She's hit a brand-new black Audi, which is completely obscured by the shade from the trees.

Michel spins around, alarmed at the sound of the collision. He doesn't immediately register the face of the driver.

The girl springs out of her 2CV: "What a stupid place to park a car!" Michel is incredulous: "What?"

"How is anyone supposed to see a black car parked in the shade?" She points at the collision. "I mean, really?"

"It was parked under a tree for ..."

Their eyes meet for the first time, a special moment: she's about five ten and slender in build. He absorbs her gentle features, slightly freckled golden skin. A certain innocence in those Arctic-blue eyes, still shiny with tears. Her blonde hair, slightly wavy, completes a picture of perfection. He's mesmerized by the girl's beauty. It disarms him, totally.

"Luckily it's only a rental!"

Michel wanders over, inspects the dented door panel, not concerned. The girl is silent, watches him, waits. She's curious. Michel glances at the 2CV appreciatively. "This is a great old car. Yours?"

She waits: "No, I borrowed it from Pascal at the Hostellerie. I'm sorry. It's just that it's normally deserted up here."

"But not today ... D'you come here often?"

"That's a corny line!"

"Yes, I know."

"Every year; the same date, June 15th. Usually with my sister, but she fell and broke her arm...a pity."

Michel wonders if he should probe: "I'm sorry. Why here?"

She wonders if she should answer: "To place flowers on our mother's memorial. This was her family's château for generations."

She turns and gently inclines her head towards it. Michel can't take his eyes off her face; and the summer dress does little to disguise her perfect figure.

"Are you thinking of buying it?"

He pauses: "I'm really not sure yet."

"I grew up here."

"Oh ... what a fabulous place to grow up."

"So will you buy it?"

"Depends."

"On what?"

"Oh, the usual. Cost, legalities, searches."

She looks at Pascal's dented bumper: "Yes of course ..." She'd almost forgotten about the collision and the flicker of a smile crosses her face.

"So, are you staying at the Hostellerie in Lignières?"

"Yes."

Michel can't believe this good fortune: "Well look, I'm staying there too. I left all my car documents in the room. Let's sort this out – over tea perhaps?"

"Yes, alright."

"Good."

"Your accent sounds, what, French-Canadian. Is that right?"

He laughs: "Yes, I am Québécois. My parents moved to New Brunswick, then Quebec from Paris before I was born. So, our accents at home were a jumble of different pronunciations. And we use different words for things back home. What I was taught at school was different to the French language my parents spoke. By the way, I'm Michel Bouchard."

The girl turns, wanders back over towards the secluded garden, calls over her shoulder, right hand on her hip, a momentary backwards glance: "So. I will collect my things. See you there, in a while."

Michel shakes his head with a grin, starts the engine, flicks the radio on. He watches her return to the memorial stones. From her bag she takes out her sunglasses and mobile phone and opens it. He reverses the car out and pulls away.

She puts on her sunglasses: "Camille? Guess what?"

Rendez-vous

Hostellerie de la Poste, Lignières-Sonneville.

THE PRIVATE GARDEN TERRACE at the Hostellerie is idyllic. Set in the centre of the small town in the heart of the Charente, it is quiet and secluded. The business is run by Pascal and Marie-Christine Couprie and advertised in the guides as 'family run.' It is modest, with home-cooked cuisine, local wines and, of course, an abundance of Cognac and Pineau. This little-known vin de liqueur is blended with one quarter of Cognac with three-quarters of other fermented grapes.

Michel sits alone at a table with a laptop, reviewing his photos: a slide show of Château Boissier and surrounding countryside; thousands of hectares of Cognac vines. He sips a chilled glass of Jules Gautret Pineau rouge and the savours exquisite taste. Unused crockery – teapot and cups – are on the table. He's simultaneously studying some mysterious German maps of the region dated 1940.

The girl comes into the garden terrace from reception, flustered and obviously late. She's changed her clothes; her hair still looks wet, quickly towel-dried. He stands courteously. "Sorry if I shouted at you earlier." She says with a smile.

"What kind of an idiot parks under a tree, huh?" He says, repeating her words and she initially makes no comment.

"I was upset, that's all. I've been trying to find out who you are ... on my laptop."

"I've told you that already." He doesn't mention she hasn't told him who she is. "A little background?"

"And?"

"Bouchard is a well-known name in Canada!"

"Are you worried about something? Come and sit down. The tea is cold and so is the Pineau, fortunately. I have to say I am a convert; Pascal says I must try it poured over freshly sliced melon."

"Um, too much sugar." She settles herself in one of the metal garden chairs: "No, I am not worried about anything. It's just people. People let me down."

"I promise – absolutely - not to be one of those people." He holds out his hand, looks her in the eyes. "We need to be formally introduced."

"You don't know?"

He's confused: "No."

"Jeanne."

"That's pretty."

"Thank you." She takes his hand and meets his gaze. There is a moment of hesitation, as if she is waiting for something: "Jeanne Boissier." She pauses, eyes him carefully as if now waiting for a reaction. When there isn't, she releases his hand slowly, but her eyes are still on him, questioning.

On the table, the Pineau sits in a chiller; her glass awaits her.

"May I pour you a glass?"

"I need to buy some cigarettes." She inclines her head towards the village. "There is a Tabac down towards the church and the old lavoir."

"Old lavoir, that's quaint." Michel dithers a moment, grabs his laptop and places it under the table out of sight. She is already moving. "I'll come with you."

"Fine." She opens the terrace garden gate onto the path beside Rue de L'Eglise. "That's the old communal place to wash your clothes, right? I've never actually seen one."

"You haven't lived, Michel." They stroll down the narrow street towards the Tabac. "Why do you want to buy the château?"

Michel's reply sounds awkward: "It ticks all the boxes."

"Il coche toutes les cases." She mimics his French-Canadian accent, a very accurate impersonation. He looks at her, impressed and intrigued. She raises her eyebrows with a smile.

Tabac

Rue de L'Eglise, Lignières-Sonneville

THE TEENAGE BOY BEHIND the counter makes no secret of drooling over Jeanne, but there's more to it than how she looks: it's as if he knows her, although there is no sign of any familiarity between them.

"Pack of Marlborough please." She looks at Michel. He shakes his head. He looks around, taps his pockets. "Oh, and a lighter."

Michel fumbles for spare change: "Actually, yeah, maybe some gum." The boy still stares at Jeanne who seems oblivious of his attention towards her. "What flavour?"

"Peppermint, please. I quit tobacco, oh, fourteen months ago. I hardly even think about it now ... fifteen months ... and three weeks."

The boy hands Michel a pack of gum, which he rips open theatrically as if desperate. Michel then offers to pay, but she has done it, already leaving, and laughing at his antics. "Small price to pay for a wrecked black Audi," she says casually.

"Yeah! You know I still crave nicotine. Crazy! Now I'm on thirty packs of gum a day. That's why I have no teeth!"

"They look real enough."

"Some of them are, yes."

As they walk out of the shop, the boy pulls out his phone and starts rapidly punching numbers. He must let his girlfriend know who he's just served. Michel doesn't notice. But Jeanne does; she is used to it.

*

Michel quickly follows her outside, onto the pavement. She lights up. "I am trying to stop." She takes a good pull, expels the smoke with relish. He watches. "But it's not easy, I know."

For a moment she frowns and then laughs again: "It's a question of wanting to."

"Or having chronic sugar addiction, like me."

"Come on, let's stroll. Pascal cannot allow smoking; it's the rules now." She takes his arm casually, like an old friend.

"Even in the garden?"

"Especially in the garden ... Parisians flaunt the rules, but not here in Segonzac. Pascal would summon the Gendarmes."

"Hah! No?"

"I'm serious; he's very pernickety about such things!" A

53

sideways glance and another delicious smile. He's enchanted by her.

They stroll off Rue de L'Eglise down to the banks of the river Collinaud.

*

Its waters run clear and deep. They find a spot and sit. Two fishermen along the bank are nonchalantly absorbed. One nudges the other. They both look at Jeanne and quickly turn back to their fishing. Michel is mystified at the exaggerated reaction of the two men. "How many other properties have you seen?" She lies back on the grass. "I, I haven't."

"You must love Château Boissier?" Jeanne extinguishes her cigarette, and carefully buries the butt deep in the mud. Michel watches her and she returns his gaze, smiles. She walks carefully down to the river and swills her fingers in the water, shakes the drops off meticulously. He joins her.

"Why is your mother's memorial in that spot?"

"It's a long story."

"I have time ... if ..." He senses there is much more she wants to tell him, so he remains silent and gives her time.

"Both my parents were killed in the fire that devastated the château." He closes his eyes, embarrassed and waits. She continues, delivering her words slowly and with thought. This is difficult for her: "It was five years ago. My sister and I were

54

rescued, but they, they died ... it was the worst night of my life. But I remember there was a beautiful young paramedic called Margot. She was very kind to my sister and me. Stayed with us for ages at the hospital in Cognac."

"That's good to hear."

"Yes. And a policeman called Gaston Leclerc. I'll never forget him either. Coming here brings it all back ... I can see their faces ... and remember the smell of smoke in the air." He feels he is walking a tightrope, having asked her such an intimate question: "I'm so sorry, Jeanne, really, I am. I feel I've pried."

"You weren't to know." He touches her arm. She looks into his eyes and sees he is uneasy. "It's okay. We only come back here once a year. It's our ritual anniversary. It's hard to do it alone."

"But you're not alone, are you?"

She places her hand on top of his, a gentle squeeze: "No, I am not." "Is that why the château hasn't been sold before? Because of the association with the tragedy? I remember a house collapsed in Quebec ... four builders were killed; buried alive. It's still empty to this day. People perceive, I don't know, that it's haunted." "Yes, I understand. Everybody knows. Try keeping a secret around here. Not so much as haunted, but unlucky."

"But you don't own it?"

"No. We had to sell it. The lawyer told us our father had incurred serious debts." "It must have been tough."

55

A very special moment; she gives him that captivating look: "You have no idea, Michel." He holds her gaze, and her hand is still on his. "What are you doing now? This afternoon?" He shakes his head perplexed: "I'm having a very wonderful time. What Trevor Howard might call 'a brief encounter'."

Jeanne seems not to have heard his witty riposte: "I mean, what would you have done if you ..."

"If you hadn't hit my car? Nothing. A bit of sightseeing, then back to Pascal's for dinner and a few glasses. Maybe even a Cognac since I'm here."

"Come on, I want to take you somewhere special."

*

Michel and Jeanne are in a small rowing boat on the river Collinaud. Charentais houses and green parkland run alongside the river. They are having a picnic. It is a blissful and idyllic scene. Fauré plays from an old radio. Classic FM.

He leans back and gazes up at the massive blue sky: "This is just perfect." "We used to come here with our mother and our Aunt Bénédicte." He waits a careful moment: "Was your mother as pretty ... as you?" She bats his arm playfully: "Prettier!" Jeanne stretches back in the boat, dreamy. He waits more than five minutes, not wanting to over-play his hand: "What was she like?" "You ask a lot of questions."

"Do I?"

"Yes."

The boat drifts on the current and she says nothing for a while. Then: "Soft, warm, kind, funny. She used to play the piano to Camille and me; and sang to us. She adored artists such as Carole King, Simon and Garfunkel. Lots of sixties songs, even Nat King Cole. Beautiful. She was so beautiful."

"I'm sure."

"She used to sing us that Beatles song with French lyric ... sont les mots qui vont très bien ensemble ... très bien ensemble ..." She starts to hum the melody then suddenly sits up; her eyes are streaming. She realises it was the song their mother had sung to them the night she died, the night of the fire.

"Jeanne, I am sorry. I shouldn't ... you said I ask a lot of questions." She composes herself: "I'm alright now ... I rather like crying, you know. It's therapeutic. Cleanses the soul."

"I'll take your word for it."

"Do you know what I would like to do now?"

Michel grins mischievously: "Thrash that old 2CV around the vineyards, park up and then drink a few glasses of Cognac Schweppes in Pascal's Garden?"

"You're a mind reader."

"I'd rather be a lip reader."

She gives him that look.

*

Michel rows the boat across the river to a wooden jetty and hands the line over to a boy, who secures it to a mooring. He too seems mesmerised by Jeanne's appearance and takes the five Euro tip without a word, his mouth open in wonder. They get out of the boat, fooling around like kids. He pretends to fall in, fakes it fabulously.

She laughs out loud: "And we haven't had a drink yet."

"I'm crazy enough sober."

She takes out her mobile and looks at the time: "I need you to meet someone." She scrolls to contacts and dials a number in Lignières-Sonneville.

Bénédicte

2, Place Emile Zola, Lignières-Sonneville.

MICHEL AND JEANNE WALK down the main road and turn off to a row of tiny quaint old cottages to number two. It has aquamarine shutters; all the rest are cream. He notices the colour difference and she picks up.

"My aunt is a bit of a rebel, like me. She should conform to the local colour but that's not her style!"

"I'd better watch it."

She knocks on the door, opens it and walks straight in: "Aunt B! It's me!" A lady's voice replies, distant: "Out in the garden as usual. It never ends!" "Wait here, Michel."

He remains as instructed, looks around the room: a clutter of bric-à-brac, memorabilia. On the wall, there are a few vintage film posters: on one of them Bénédicte Boissier is clearly the star. He walks over to a sideboard, decorated with art deco porcelain and silverware. He sees an empty bottle of Cognac and reads the label:

59

1858 NAPOLEON 111 EMPEREUR 37% Vol.

For a moment Michel does a double take. It was the year the Cognac house of A. E. Dor was founded; and when the bottle was full would have been priceless. How on earth did Jeanne's aunt come by it?

Then he spots a wedding photograph. He picks it up, intrigued and studies the expressionless faces; they don't reflect a joyous occasion. In the centre of the image are the bride and groom: an indignant looking, much younger Jeanne and a toughly built man, much older. His features are southern-European and his dark eyes stare into the camera. Beside Jeanne are clearly Pascal and Marie-Christine. And, next to them a young blonde girl, her face turned sharply away from the photographer's lens.

Michel stands so absorbed that he fails to notice Jeanne and her aunt Bénédicte standing there, watching him curiously.

"Yes, I'm married."

He is manifestly disappointed and can't hide it: "It was too good to be true, I suppose. Far too good."

She replaces her wedding ring, her eyes glistening with tears: "To a man I have absolutely nothing in common with. But he saved my life and I suppose he is kind in his own way." He watches her twist the gold band onto her finger. She grimaces: "I take it off as soon as I walk into the secluded garden at the château and my mother's memorial stone. I'm ..." She is choking on her own words.

He waits, replaces the photograph. She catches his eye. "I'm trapped."

He watches her carefully, eggshells: "Yes, I see now."

"Do you?"

"Yes, otherwise he'd be here to support you...today of all days ... since your sister is out of action, so to speak."

"You are kind."

"But I am right, aren't I? You must tell me the reason why another time." He pauses and looks at her aunt. "Are you going to introduce us?"

Michel glances at the elderly lady with a smile. She's dressed in black but wearing red rubber gardening gloves.

"Sorry, this is my aunt Bénédicte."

The old lady wiggles the fingers of her rubber gloves in greeting. They speak in a rapid Charentais patois which Michel can't follow.

"She says her hands are too frail and she finds it hard to get them off, to shake hands."

"I see." Michel smiles charmingly, glances at the film posters: "You, Madame?" Bénédicte nods; her face breaks into a crinkly old smile: "The swinging sixties, yes! Very swinging! The producer was a man called Louis Doupeux. I may have mentioned him?" Jeanne looks confused: "No, I don't think so, B. Not that I remember." A mischievous twinkle: "Oh, thought I had."

Jeanne and Bénédicte exchange some more rapid words, peck one another on the cheek three or four times and then leave.

*

Once outside they walk back in the direction from which they'd come. The atmosphere between them is brittle.

Jeanne breaks the ice: "I have all the money in the world, but no happiness. Absolutely none whatsoever.

"That's sad, Jeanne."

"I had to find a way to tell you, Michel. And going to see Bénédicte seemed like the best way. I called her when we left the boat ... just to check she was in."

"And I am glad you did."

"Will you listen?"

"Of course, I will."

"Aunt Bénédicte likes you. That's what we were talking about when we left her house."

"She's a fine judge of character, that Aunt Bénédicte."

Her sad face melts into a smile: "She is very special; it means everything." Jeanne wipes her face with her hands, relieved, the load is shared. Spontaneously they stop walking. She stands on tiptoes and kisses his cheek. He wipes her tears, and she says his name softly: "Michel ..."

"Yes, I know ... I think I'm beginning to understand."

"Some of it, maybe."

They hold hands and walk, her head tilted against his shoulder. They stroll together out of Lignières and up to the vineyards. Thousands of hectares – as far as the eye can see – of symmetrical Cognac vines. The air is still, the sun shines, a panoramic blue sky, an idyllic scene, for this is a couple on the brink of falling in love.

Candlelight

*Hostellerie de la Poste,
Lignières-Sonneville, Charente*

MICHEL AND JEANNE ARE sitting at a candlelit table on the
garden terrace, with a bottle of white Burgundy, plates, and a
basket of bread. They are laughing and joking. A local French radio
station plays classic songs in the background. Once again, the
scene is tranquil and idyllic.

*

In the kitchen of the Hostellerie, Pascal and Marie-Christine
look out of the kitchen window into the garden at the happy
couple. Pascal does not look happy; Marie-Christine is curious.
Pascal says: "What do you think? I don't like him."

She is more reasonable: "I'm not quite sure what I think. But I
know I've never seen her look so happy."

"An open mind then, Marie-Christine." A touch of sarcasm.

"I've told you what I think. Don't be so miserable and judgmental ... and stop looking at me like that. I've seen that expression before."

*

Back out in the garden Jeanne and Michel hear a song on the radio; soft and sexy. "Come on, I love this tune ... let's dance."

He stands, takes her hand.

"So do I, yes."

He takes her in his arms – as he has longed to do all day – and they dance. The atmosphere is magical: the garden, the terrace, coloured lights. All the revelations at aunt Bénédicte's house are forgotten; or at least they are put on hold. They dance to the music, initially hesitant, then close, her head on his shoulder. Her arms are wrapped around him. They both have their eyes closed, dancing as one.

*

At the kitchen window, Marie-Christine stands alone, watching the scene with undisguised pleasure. She says to herself: "Now I know exactly what I think. And I don't blame you, Jeanne. Not at all. Monsieur Bouchard is charming." She chuckles quietly to herself. If she wasn't happily married, she easily could fall for him herself.

*

Later that night at the foot of the stairs in the hallway, Jeanne climbs up slowly, the briefest of glances over her shoulder at Michel, who is standing there. She opens one of the two bedroom doors and goes in. Pascal emerges from the kitchen and coughs discreetly, looking at Michel with contempt.

"Breakfast, tomorrow, monsieur Bouchard?" He gazes up at Jeanne's bedroom door as it clicks shut. Pascal doesn't hear it being locked from the inside. He shakes his head; he's nothing more than an interfering busybody; Michel picks up.

"Just coffee and juice, please. I don't suppose you serve pancakes and maple syrup, do you?"

"No, monsieur, we don't." His tone implies: this is rural France, not New York. Michel grins: "Good night, Pascal. Thank your wife for dinner. We really enjoyed the pan-fried veal and potatoes. And please thank her for lending us the radio. The music made all the difference to our evening."

Pascal huffs goodnight as Michel climbs the stairs. He watches for a moment, and then turns off all the downstairs lights. The bar door closes with finality.

Michel is now outside her door, about to knock, but he can't. His hand edges slowly to the doorknob. Still, he can't. He creeps back to his own door, stops. Opens it, waits. Walks back towards Jeanne's door. A creaky floorboard suddenly squeaks. It sounds like a mistuned violin. No! He stops on a dime, indecision written

66

all over his face. He can't do it, even though he wants to, but he can't. He turns and slopes off back to his room.

*

Behind her closed bedroom door Jeanne sits on her bed, staring at the door, just hoping it will open. Nervous expectation is written all over her face and she's wringing her hands anxiously ... there is no sign of her wedding band on the nightstand, just her earrings, bracelet and phone.

*

Downstairs, Marie-Christine emerges from the shadows into the hallway, a shaft of outside light shines in. She looks satisfied at what she has seen and follows her husband to their bedroom on the ground floor.

*

The following morning Michel opens his bedroom door and comes out onto the sun-drenched landing of the Hostellerie. He's bright and breezy; another beautiful day in the Poitou Charentes. He wanders over to Jeanne's bedroom door, hesitates, thinks better of it and charges down the stairs to the breakfast room, empty. He walks to the bar, which is also empty. Then to the reception desk. He dings the bell. Two children appear their heads just above the counter. They make a rude face at Michel. He makes a rude face back; they giggle mischievously.

A few moments later Pascal appears, wiping his mouth with a

serviette, shoos the kids away. They want to stay and have fun with this new stranger. He seems to have a sense of humour, unlike their Papa. Michel can't hide his anxiety.

"Where's Jeanne?

"Gone."

He's shocked: "Gone? When?"

"Oh ... Early this morning." Pascal glances at his watch and stifles a yawn. "Very early. Sorry. I took her to the railway station at Jarnac."

Michel shakes his head: "Where did she go?"

"Back to Paris, of course." There's a slight tone of self-satisfaction in his reply. He wants to say back to her husband, but he dare not incur the wrath of Marie-Christine. She seems to approve of this Canadian being friendly with their precious Jeanne. He certainly does not. Michel shrugs, manifestly disappointed. He turns to leave: "Thanks anyway, Pascal." There is an air of schadenfreude in the look Pascal gives Michel's retiring back.

*

Michel ducks out of reception, heads for his car. Out in the rear garden of the Hostellerie, Marie-Christine is feeding two dogs. She looks up at him. Her smile borders on flirtation: "Let me make you some breakfast, Monsieur Bouchard. Fresh coffee? Juice? There's fresh bread from the village boulangerie; croissants; our home-

68

made strawberry conserve ... I can boil you a couple of eggs."

He sounds fed up: "Thanks all the same, but I've lost my appetite." She stands up from the dog's bowl and smoothes down her pinafore: "Are you alright?" He places his laptop and a small suitcase on a garden table; he needs to talk: "To be perfectly honest, yesterday I thought I had met the woman I was destined to marry. A chance encounter. But today ..."

Marie-Christine absorbs the honesty of his words: "But Jeanne has already been married, monsieur ... for some time."

"I know." He couldn't look more dejected and forlorn. "I'm sorry, I shouldn't be discussing such ..." He quickly picks up his belongings and turns to leave. Marie-Christine watches him very carefully and decides: "Wait a moment, please." Michel flicks the car's remote, opens the door. She comes over with a conspiratorial look about her:

"What exactly did Jeanne say to you?"

He takes a cautious moment to respond: "A lot of things; that she was unhappy." "Anything else ... about her?"

He brightens: "She took me to meet her aunt Bénédicte. Which felt like a privilege ... she was quite charming to me."

Marie-Christine looks surprised, shocked even at this revelation. She looks him up and down as if weighing him up, assessing the sincerity of his words.

"She took you there, why?"

"She wanted to find a way to tell me her ... situation. So as not to mislead me and give me false hope. I am not sure."

"Look, Jeanne is my best friend, even though she ... even though she's a ..." This is clearly difficult for her, impossible at this moment. "Pascal and I have known her since school. We care about her. We've known her forever."

"So do I ... and I didn't even know her twenty-four hours ago."

He dumps his luggage on the passenger seat and walks around the car, about to get in. "Wait a moment. Don't go yet, please."

Michel shrugs as Marie-Christine dashes into reception, picks up the phone, punches numbers. She watches him. Michel kicks a tyre absent-mindedly, looks at the dented panel and smiles. He can hear her voice in his head so clearly: Who would park a black car in the shade? If any other person had said that to him, he would have ranted. But he didn't. He found the whole encounter funny.

Marie-Christine is in an animated discussion, continually looking out of the window at Michel. Then she scribbles on a notepad, dashes back out to him and hands him the note: "Go to her. Follow your heart. This will help you."

Michel looks at the hastily-scribbled note. She explains: "Camille is her sister. She can easily contact Jeanne later today."

"Why? Why are you doing this?"

She smiles: "Because I can see you make her happy ... and she's had years of, well, she told you, I'm sure."

Michel spontaneously pecks her on the cheek: "Thank you." He gets into his car and swings out of the car park.

*

Marie-Christine wanders back into Reception to find Pascal, looking very annoyed: "What was all that about?" He asks her with a distinct attitude.

"I called Camille on her mobile. She was just on her way to the shop." Pascal looks confused now: "What? Why?"

She turns and looks at him: "You know why. We know why. And because I can see he loves her. It's in his eyes."

Pascal's attitude is dismissive: "Pah! After one night?"

She narrows her eyes: "But that's just it, isn't it? There wasn't a night. He didn't go in. He respected her."

Pascal again: "How do you know?"

She laughs: "Same as you. I waited and watched."

"He nearly went in."

She huffs: "Yes, he nearly went in, but he didn't. Goodness me, you're so stupid sometimes, Pascal." She pauses: "No, you are so stupid most of the time. Grrrr!" With that she hurries into the kitchen to make coffee. She's tempted to slam the door but decides not to.

The two dogs wander into Reception to Pascal for attention. He crouches down and makes a fuss of them: 'She's always damn well right ... isn't she, boys? Oh well, best get used to it after all these years. Come on, I need to smoke a crafty cheroot!"

Headline

SNCF Railway Station, Jarnac, Charente

MICHEL CATCHES THE TGV just in time; Paris Montparnasse via Angoulême. The ticket office in Jarnac had only two people waiting in the queue, and he was quickly able to get a first-class ticket. The double-decker train is full of commuters; well-dressed businesspeople all busily working on their laptops or mobiles. The atmosphere is hushed and incredibly civilized.

He chooses an upper-level window seat, relishing the air-conditioned carriage and watching the green fields of the Charente countryside flash by. He's served petit déjeuner by a pleasant cabin attendant: coffee, juice, croissant, and a cold bottle of Evian. Michel dabs his lip with a napkin and wonders how his day will turn out.

He settles comfortably, ready to enjoy the journey, then something catches his eye on the opposite seat. A folded Le Monde newspaper photo reveals a photograph of half of a woman's face.

He leans over, grabs it and turns it over. The headline reads:

Festival De Cannes. Jeanne Rey:
La Nouvelle Icône Du Cinéma Français

There is no question it's Jeanne and the photo captures her beauty. The new icon of French Cinema. She's a film star. More than that: a celebrity! And he hadn't even recognized her.

Worse, he'd never heard of her. He thumps back against the headrest in disbelief at his naivety: So, why is she not Jeanne Boissier? Not that it matters; she's obviously using a stage name to dissociate herself from her roots.

It's no wonder everybody has been behaving so strangely – the kid in the Tabac in Lignières – the two fishermen – Aunt Bénédicte – Pascal and Marie-Christine. In a way, they were all protecting her; and she'd said nothing herself. Why? Modesty? He's considering these options when suddenly a bleep jolts him back into reality. He takes out his i-pod and it flicks to FaceTime.

Caller/Message ID: Noah Gagnon at Piermaster Corporation, Quebec, Canada. The phone screen shows the image of Noah Gagnon. He has silver-grey hair; rugged good looks and his tone is assertive.

Gagnon is clearly the boss:

"Mike. Vous avez trouvé le moulin?"

74

("Mike, have you found the windmill yet?")

Michel tries to sound casual:

"Non, pas encore."

("No, not yet.")

"Formidable. Alors, pas de Cognac?"

("Great. So, no Cognac?")

"Non."

("No.")

Gagnon's tone is lurching towards impatience:

"Et le château Boissier?"

("And the château Boissier?")

Je vais peute-être finir par l'acheter."

("I may end up actually buying it.")

"Bon. Le Cognac vaut dix fois plus."

("Good. The Cognac is worth ten châteaux.")

Michael injects positivity into proceedings:

"Je ferai avancer les négociations,"

("I'll advance negotiations.")

There is a pause as Gagnon considers:

"Mais enfin, où êtes-vous?"

("Where the hell are you?")

"Dans le TGV pour Paris."

("On the TGV to Paris.")

Gagnon sounds astonished to hear this revelation.

"Paris? Pourquoi?"

("Paris? Why?")

"Je suis une piste. Il faut que je trouve qui sont les propriétaires du château."

("I'm following a lead. I need to find out who owns the château.")

Gagnon: "Ne dépensez pas trop de mon argent là-dessus. Réglez ça en vitesse."

("Don't spend too much of my money. Wrap it up quickly.")

The line goes dead; the screen goes blank; he makes a face. He picks up the newspaper again, stares at Jeanne's photograph and reads the article once more. He still can't believe what he is seeing and who she really is.

Camille

Confiserie Boissier,
40 Rue du Poitou, 75003, Paris

THE BACK DOOR OF a Mercedes limousine is held open for Jeanne by a chauffeur. She gets out and ducks quickly into her sister's shop. The chauffeur looks left and right, as he has been trained to do; fans and paparazzi are everywhere because of her new film. He gets back behind the wheel and waits. Sometimes she's quick, other times slow. He's learned to be patient: Jeanne Rey is never predictable, and her mood swings are legendary.

*

Inside the confiserie, Jeanne's twin sister Camille is waiting to greet her. She looks the same as Jeanne except half of her face is disfigured with the scars of burns from the fire at the château. The two of them embrace, but Camille senses Jeanne is short of time and she knows – or can guess – the reason why.

"How is your arm, Camille?"

She winces in pain: "My collar bone is fractured too. The doctor explained it all when she showed me the X-Ray; well, the on-screen picture. No film now; I didn't realise." Jeanne frowns in sympathy: "No wonder you are in so much pain, Camille. A train journey would have been miserable. I take it they gave you pain relief?" Camille nods, wanting to move on and stands back to look at her sister: "Well, how did it go ... without me?" The last two words are delivered with a sense of humour. She brushes her sister's face affectionately.

And Jeanne touches her hand lovingly: "Oh, same as usual, I suppose. Going there always affects me deeply, as it does you. Time and place. Memories." Jeanne pauses. "But I met someone there. A chance encounter."

"Hmm, you said as much on the phone. Tell me all. I've been waiting for this with bated breath!"

Jeanne gives her a brief overview of what happened in the secluded garden; from the car 'accident' – to Aunt Bénédicte – the boat trip – and dinner on the terrace at the Hostellerie. Oh, and his name is Michel from Quebec. She describes him in excruciating detail, which amuses Camille, since her sister hasn't been enthused by any man for years. Camille is surprised: "I wonder if it's wise to sell our château now, Jeanne."

"Why? You said that the shop was prospering these days?"

Camille looks around at the chilled glass cabinets displaying handcrafted confectionery: bonbons, chocolate-covered marzipan,

Turkish delight, and caramel shortbread; mouth watering delicacies: "Oh, it's not so bad ... I get by."

Jeanne looks at her with an air of frustration; she has her reasons: "We never go home these days, except on the anniversary. Our solitary asset consists of a dormant property which we can't even rent out because it's so dilapidated. Carlo's opinion is that ..." Camille interrupts her: "I really don't care what Carlo thinks ... it's none of his business. As I understand it, the property is held in trust until we reach twenty-five. Then we have the option to do whatever we want with it. Our decision."

Jeanne's expression becomes bleaker and bleaker: "That's the problem though, isn't it, Camille? Since the fire everything is to do with him. Everything is his business. At the time he had power of attorney over us because of our age – and there was no one else – was there? Even Aunt Bénédicte wanted nothing to do with two rebellious teenagers. And you were moodier than me."

"Ha!"

"True!"

Camille laughs at the untruth and then, after a moment, becomes serious: "What do you mean, Jeanne? The château belongs to us, doesn't it?"

"I'm not sure. Since I was, what, obliged, compelled to marry Carlo, he manages all my financial affairs. He said I was incompetent with money."

Camille is wary: "But the château is independent from your

marital affairs and finances; it's ours, isn't it?"

"I don't know." Jeanne looks around the beautiful shop. "It's like this place. Your name might be on the lease, but I bet Fieschi owns the freehold. He and his Corsican friends probably own the street ... the whole of Paris." They both laugh again, but Camille hasn't heard her sister describe her husband by his surname since their wedding day. The two sisters regard one another with mutual understanding.

"I must go. I'll see you tomorrow. Don't forget the thing with the spare key, will you?" A peck on the cheek and Jeanne is out of the shop and back in the waiting limo before the rain starts falling across Paris in sheets. As she clips on her seatbelt, she remembers the word she used to Michel when describing her marriage: Piégé.

Trapped.

"Rue Guénégaud, Miss Rey?"

Jeanne sighs: "Yes, I suppose so." She settles back and watches Parisians struggling with their umbrellas as the heavens open.

Home

Rue Guénégaud, Paris

THE SOLID OLD APARTMENT block in the Monnaie quarter of Paris oozes opulence and class. Even in torrential rain. Outside it a dozen paparazzi wait, hungry, disparate predators with their cameras and gigantic parasols.

Jeanne's limousine pulls up. The concierge from the block comes out of the building with two security men. He's an older man in a braided uniform. Once again, Jeanne emerges from the rear door, helped by the chauffeur who holds a large umbrella over her. The paparazzi call out to her en masse, pleading: 'Smile, Jeanne! Just one picture! Please! ... How about a quote? ...'

She ducks under the umbrella to get out of the rain.

More commotion from journalists: '*Un Seul Billet*' had great reviews in Cannes ... any comment ... oh, please, Jeanne ... just one quote.'

The pack moves in towards her. Cameras flash in the rain and turmoil.

*

Inside the marble-tiled lobby of the building, Jeanne is brushing rain off her raincoat. She's had enough. She takes off her sunglasses.

"Bastards!"

The old concierge, shocked at her expletive, summons the lift: "Without them, you are no one. It is the way, Madame."

"I was someone, without them. I'm not so sure anymore, Monsieur Fournier. Really, I'm not."

He bides his time, waiting for the lift, looking up at the old storey-indicator dial as the open metal cage descends from the top floor. It seems to take forever. Jeanne continues: "Not that I'm ungrateful, Monsieur Fournier. Really, I'm not. But after the phone hacking scandal I even feel sorry for Prince Harry! ... When that photojournalist fell out of a tree in Saint-Tropez, I almost wet myself with laughter ... oops, sorry." Fournier hides his shock: "No matter, Madame. Oh, Monsieur Fieschi arrived about an hour ago, Madame."

Her heart sinks. Bang goes some time to myself, for a change. She gets into the old Otis lift; he closes the steel gates with a crash. It rises slowly. She takes a powder compact out of her bag and looks at herself in the mirror, tidying her hair. "How marvellous it is to be back in this place." She struggles out of her damp raincoat and folds it over her arm as the old lift jolts to a sudden stop.

*

Jeanne gets out with a deep sigh; her mind is in turmoil. She lets herself into the elegant old apartment with eleven-foot ceilings and decoratively painted cornices. The lavishly appointed lounge has an abundance of expensive furniture, antique artefacts, and floor-to ceiling silk drapes. She throws her raincoat onto a chair, frustrated. She just doesn't want to be there. Her heart is still in the Charente with Michel, sitting in the garden at the Hostellerie, drinking Pineau. And dancing.

Her husband, Carlo Fieschi stands up to greet her. He's well-dressed, well-coiffured and well-fed. He's clearly been reading an assortment of newspapers, including LE MONDE. The same 'Jeanne in Cannes' feature that Michel read on the TGV. The lounge is decked out with flowers. Fieschi smiles charmingly: "Welcome home, Jeanne. So how was your annual pilgrimage to the château with Camille?"

"Fine, thank you, Carlo. Except Camille wasn't able to come, because of her arm. And collar bone, so it turns out."

"Ah yes, I had quite forgotten." But his expression says he hadn't.

She looks surprised at the sight of the flowers, verging on suspicious. He immediately picks up: "A little welcome home for you, my dear."

"I've only been gone two days ... I think I might take a bath and ..." But he cuts her off ungraciously and opens the dining room doors to reveal a beautifully decorated table: crystal glasses and an ice bucket containing a bottle of Bollinger. "Signora Palledri has prepared her signature dish: tortellini de ricotta, followed by turbot with basil. I believe it used to be one of your favourites ... and mine." Jeanne tries to look enthusiastic, but fails: "Oh . . . I can see she has been to a great deal of trouble, Carlo. I don't really know what to say."

"You mean, not without a script to read from?" He tries to sound ironic and amusing, but his retort falls flat. She bites her tongue and ignores him. But Fieschi ploughs on. "Champagne. The finest bottle of Chianti. And Panettone for dessert." Then he stops suddenly. "What were you going to say, my dear? With my enthusiasm to please you – as a welcome home - I interrupted you."

Jeanne sighs at his attempt to spoil her: "No, no. I just thought I'd take a bath. All the travelling has worn me out."

Fieschi's smile betrays his inner feelings: She caught a first-class train from Jarnac to Paris – and probably slept the whole journey – then my chauffeur collected her from Montparnasse station. And then drove her to her sister's shop. How can she possibly be tired? She's twenty-one years old and has everything life has to offer. But his reply is "Of course, my darling Jeanne. How long do you need?"

84

She flashes her famous smile: "Oh! No more than an hour, I guess. Maybe two, actually." Just as Jeanne turns and leaves the room, Signora Palledri, a middle-aged Italian woman enters and raises her eyebrows with undisguised annoyance: "Prima donna, Signor Fieschi?"

"No! Madame is just tired after a long, demanding day. June is never a good month for her." Fieschi explains to her in fluent Italian; he's keen to put the record straight.

"Oh," says the Signora, unconvinced.

*

Jeanne walks out of the lounge and into the hallway. She looks at her reflection in an ornate gilt mirror. She looks tired: grey rings beneath her eyes and pale skin. Her hair is a mess from the rain and travel. She'd not had time to shower when she left the Hostellerie earlier with Pascal. Slowly she removes her bracelet, watch and finally her wedding ring. She twists it off awkwardly as if wanting to be disassociated from it.

She walks from the hallway through to the bedroom's en-suite taking off her clothes as she progresses into the bathroom and starts filling the bath. She clicks on the radio; the same tune as she danced to with Michel the night before.

*

Fieschi moves silently and cautiously out of the lounge into the hallway, clutching a mobile. He puts his ear to the bedroom door and hears Jeanne singing and the running bath water. He walks into his study where a large ornate chessboard dominates the room. He dials a number from his contacts and waits:

"Antonelli ... it's me. I want to know everything about the château, yes. I want to know who has viewed it and any questions they may have asked ... no, there is no problem. Call me back."

He waits for five minutes and Fieschi is not a man given to waiting. Finally, Antonelli calls him back: "Michel Bouchard ... Quebec, huh? Find out all you can about him. Oh, and not a word to anyone, huh? This matter is only between you and me." Fieschi pauses and smiles to himself. "Send someone over to the Hostellerie de la Poste ... Find out if there was anyone else staying there besides my wife, that is. There are only two bedrooms. Pascal could use some extra money. Offer him five hundred Euros, but not while his wife's within earshot." Fieschi hangs up. Instinct and that Machiavellian cunning have made him a wealthy man. It never fails him.

*

Jeanne is in the bath. Her eyes are closed, the bubbles cover her body and her hair floats on the surface. Music plays softly in the background. Her breaths are deep; her eyelids flutter as she sleeps. Her slumber is troubled; it always is when she returns from the Charente to Paris ...

The faces of her mother and father – Edith and Gérard – haunt her dreams. Then a white space. A chessboard comes flying

86

towards her, gathering speed, spinning, rotating fast. As it's about to smash into her face, a torrent of flames suddenly explodes into a blaze and engulfs the château. Her nightmare is painfully vivid. Jeanne rolls her head from side to side, reflecting her inner turmoil. Then suddenly, it's peaceful. In her mind she sees their childhood handprints on the wall of the Cognac chais; hers and Camille's. She feels herself smile in her sleep, then she opens her eyes, shocked. For ten seconds she doesn't know where she is. Or even who she is.

Confiserie

40 Rue du Poitou, 75003, Paris

MICHEL WALKS FROM MONTPARNASSE station to the Marais district. He had been told earlier it's about an hour on foot. But the sights, sounds and smells distract him as he progresses. The walk takes him to Le Jardin du Luxembourg, past the Sorbonne, through the Latin Quarter and over the Seine at Pont Saint-Michel and Pont au Change. And, although he's been there before visiting his mother's relatives, the city is still thrilling to behold. Michel wanders around the quaint local shops, hotels, bars and cafés. He's ambling, killing time before the agreed time of his meeting. He consults Marie-Christine's note with the address. Finally, he finds an elegant Confiserie – Confectioner's – situated between a café and a craft shop.

Confiserie Boissier

He opens a thick plate glass door and enters the sweetly

smelling shop. The woman behind the counter watches him carefully. He's shocked. Half of her face resembles that of Jeanne, the other half is scarred; blemished by burn marks, possibly? It's weird and initially disturbing. He thinks of the photo in the newspaper article that is now in his jacket pocket: the photo reveals half of a woman's face. To him, at that moment, the irony is powerful. Her left arm is in a cast as he expected.

She utters one word: "Michel?"

He nods, acknowledges her arm: "Yes. Hello, Camille. I'm sorry about your arm."

"Jeanne's description of you was perfect."

"I'm not sure if that's good or bad."

She looks him up and down: "I'm not sure that it matters, to be frank." She then produces a door key which she holds out for him to take: "You are to return here at 18.30hrs, let yourself in and wait upstairs." She points at a small door behind which he assumes will be a staircase. "Fortunately, I close earlier today."

Michel walks over to the counter to take the key from her: "Thanks, Camille. Um, can't we just have a ... chat ... to ...?"

"What would you like to have a chat about? You have come here to collect a key and I have just given it to you." She waves her free arm around: "And, as you can see, I'm working."

He nods to show he understands, even though the shop is bereft of customers: "Yes, but what if I come back in a while?"

Camille puts her index finger to her lips and shakes her head. He gets the message and drops the key into his jacket pocket with finality.

Michel walks back onto Rue du Poitou feeling mildly affronted at her attitude towards him. Why? Jealousy? Disapproval? In the end he decides it doesn't matter. He has the key. Now all he must do is kill time for yet another four hours. What will he do?

Mansion

Rue Guénégaud, 75006, Paris

NOT FAR WAY FROM Michel, just steps from the Seine and the Ile de la Cité, Carlo and Jeanne are struggling to make conversation. He's mixed Martini cocktails although she hasn't touched her drink yet. Her mind is elsewhere. He has been talking about investing in an art gallery in the highly sought-after area of Saint-Germain-des-Prés just a short distance away.

"So, what do you think, my dear?" Fieschi asks his wife politely.

"I'm really not sure, Carlo. It's your business."

"But you must have an opinion, surely?"

She stands suddenly: "I'm thinking of going to see Camille later ... this evening at about six-thirty."

Fieschi sips his Martini cocktail coolly without expression: "But you saw her this morning, did you not? On the way back from the station. Luigi said he had to wait for you on Rue du Poitou. He nearly got a parking ticket."

Jeanne smoothes her dress down nervously: "Very briefly, yes. The shop was busy."

"What's wrong, Jeanne? You seem a little more on edge than normal?"

"Nothing." She almost snaps.

Fieschi frowns in disbelief: "Camille's arm will heal itself without you, my dear. Besides, I thought you have a TV show to do later this evening?"

"And so I have, yes."

As she turns to leave, his arm shoots out and grabs her waist: "I'm not going to lose you, Jeanne. Make no mistake. Whatever you're playing at."

"I'm not playing at anything." She releases herself from his grip and scurries out of the room, annoyed: what does he know?

Once Jeanne is out of earshot, Fieschi takes out his mobile: "Watch the shop all evening. I want to know exactly who comes and goes ... except for Camille, of course. I want to know the moment anything or anyone ..."

He terminates his call the moment Jeanne comes back into the lounge, in a rush: "I'll get a taxi to Camille's; or walk if it's stopped raining. And I'll call Luigi after the show. Don't wait up."

Before he can reply she is gone, but Fieschi thinks to himself: Don't worry, Luigi will know where you are ... every step of the way ... and so will I.

Liaison

40 Rue du Poitou, Paris

MICHEL IS IN AN upstairs stockroom-cum-lounge above the Confiserie. He'd let himself in earlier with the key Camille had given him. He's uneasy about the nature of his clandestine liaison with Jeanne ... and yet ...

He opens the bottle of cheap Côtes du Rhône he'd he bought from a corner shop and pours himself a generous measure into a glass tumbler: Dutch courage? On a bed settee he sits, absent-mindedly watching TV with no sound, flicking channels, waiting. He hears the ting of the bell as the shop door opens and the stairs being softly mounted ... He looks up and Jeanne is there ...

She takes his breath away: those blue eyes and gentle features; slightly freckled golden skin; and her wavy blonde hair, worn long, looks perfect. She wears a white silk dress, décolleté. The lustrous fabric clings to her gluteal muscles like a second skin, complementing her natural curves as she closes the door and walks towards him.

"You ran away," is all he can think of to say at first.

"I hated to leave, but I had to."

"I realize that."

"There are so many problems, Michel; it's so difficult."

"Let me help you solve them."

Her face appears silently on screen promoting her new film. They both stare at the feature, transfixed. He's not surprised: "I must have watched this trailer half a dozen times this evening," he says with a grin. "She's quite a girl, this Jeanne Rey."

That smile, once again: "Oh ... When did you find out?"

"On the train; a newspaper feature all about you in Cannes. Why didn't you tell me who you were?"

She laughs: "I should be offended you didn't already know!"

"Us Canadians don't get out much," he grins again, hoping to get away with it. "Alright, I'll buy that."

"Good. It's true."

"You look like you're telling the truth." She pauses. "What happened in Lignières between us happened because you wanted me. Not because of who or what I am. Me. The real me."

"And I love the real you, Jeanne," he says with feeling. "Meeting you like that was magical. There is no other word to describe it."

"You don't know the real me though," she says guardedly. "Do you?"

"But I want to. Help me find her ... come over here and I'll make a start ..." She lifts her dress, straddles his body, and kisses him like there's no tomorrow. No inhibitions now for either of them. Their passion overwhelms them in a frenzy of lovemaking. It's instant and mutual. After, they lie back on the settee, soft and silent, as the TV flickers on them. He strokes her face, she smiles, a million diamonds. They can't believe it's happened.

"We didn't even unfold the bed settee," he says mischievously.

"There was no time, was there?" She waits a few moments as he caresses her. "I think we were both in a hurry ... I was, at least. I've longed for that moment all day. But I never expected it to be so ... so intense, did you?"

"No."

She sighs in frustration: "What a nuisance I have to do a TV show later." She glances at her watch. "I need some water. You've made me thirsty, I'm breathless." Jeanne stands, pulls her dress back down, and walks across to the refrigerator in the kitchenette and opens the door.

"Have some of this warm red wine from the supermarket. It has a marvellous bouquet. Château Vinaigrette."

"No thank you, Michel ... though you make it sound so appealing." She returns with a small bottle of Evian, twists the top and has a sip. "That's better." She sits back down beside him. "You

96

look as if you want to ask me something ... I'm becoming accustomed to that expression."

"What happened to Camille's face?"

"It happened in the fire at the château. I'll tell you everything one day, I promise." She sips more water from the bottle: "The story defined our lives ... the course of it." "Whenever you're ready ... stand up a minute." He opens out the bed settee and throws a single sheet over it. She spontaneously unzips her dress and it drops to the floor; she shivers theatrically, wrapping her arms around herself.

"I thought you were in a hurry?"

She ignores the question: "Brr ... I'm chilly ... warm me up, quickly." Michel rapidly undresses and they scamper under the sheet together naked; he wraps his arms around her body, enveloping her: "That feels better," she says with a sigh. "Much, much better. He kisses her mouth and neck. She groans with pleasure, whispering his name over and over.

"You're exquisite, Jeanne, in every way."

"Don't stop whatever you're doing ... I could get used to this," Jeanne says dreamily. "Then don't go."

"You know I have to, Michel."

"Shame."

"Why?"

"Well, quite apart from ..." he says slowly.

"Yes ..."

"Well, quite apart from ..." he says again.

"Yes." She wriggles around as he strokes her bare skin lovingly, tracing his index finger from under her chin, down her body. She shivers at his very touch. "Ooh, that feels very tempting ... apart from what ..."

"I think you are an extraordinary girl, Jeanne: interesting, mischievous, intelligent, beautiful and ..."

"Yes?"

"Unpredictable; that's for sure."

"Am I?"

"Yes and passionate."

"You make me so," she says softly and pauses. "I bet you've had plenty of passion in your time, monsieur?" Suddenly she is serious.

"A cornucopia ... a profusion ... an abundance. Let's try and remember, um .... such a long list."

"Ha! I'm being serious."

"So am I." He says with a grin that dimples his cheeks.

"I mean somebody special in say, Toronto? Quebec?"

"There was."

She gives him that look and nudges him playfully: "Was she prettier than me?" "No one's prettier than you, Jeanne. Although, come to think of it, there was a girl ... 'Summer of '69'".

She laughs: "You weren't even born then, you fool!"

"It's a song, Bryan Adams."

"Who? I've never heard of him."

"He's a world-famous Canadian musician."

"Famous all over Canada, you mean?"

"No, the world."

"Still never heard of him."

"Then I rest my case ... he's an icon, just like you!"

"Touché, Monsieur."

They fall silent for a moment, savouring the intimacy and enjoying their banter. He sits up and looks her in the eye:

"Jeanne, say I were to buy the château, would you help me to restore it? Then marry me and live with me in it? Have children and live happily ever after."

The question shocks her: "I'm already married. You know that." Her eyes look sad and he waits before he answers.

"But you're here with me now."

"I know. I ... I ..."

Michel stands to fetch his glass of wine: "You told me you were unhappy. I'll never forget how you phrased it."

She looks at him, her eyes wide: "I know and I am."

"Trapped was the word you used. It was devastating to hear."

"I know what word I used, Michel. I do."

"Then let me un-trap you."

"I can't. Don't you see?"

Michel sips his glass of warm wine: "Ugh, this is awful ... because you feel you owe the man who saved your life? And your sister's too. I can see that, yes. But if you don't love him, what's the point in carrying on? Perpetuating your unhappiness?" "It's not that easy."

He discards his glass and borrows her water: "Why isn't it easy? Please tell me." Jeanne leans forward on the verge of tears. Michel touches his forehead with hers. She's trembling: "I can't, Michel. Not yet."

He pulls away, wipes her tears: "I'm in love with you, Jeanne." He pauses; he doesn't want to make her feel awkward. "I want to know − need to know - if you think we have a future together. That's all ... nobody should be trapped."

Her face and her eyes are intense as he continues: "I don't care that you are the iconic film star of Cannes. I don't even care about Fieschi. It's you. Only you. It's only you that matters to me now. I can't turn away, not after tonight. Not after this, here, now." A glimmer of a smile, because she feels it too, and he knows she does: "I know we must find a way, Michel. I do ... I do."

Michel is suddenly cautious: "Would you go back to the château, Jeanne? Or rather, would you want to go back?"

She bites her lip and thinks of the Cognac chais. The flat stone wall, two children's handprints of white paint, a left and a right.

She remembers the intense feeling she experienced that day. Was her father with her there? Was it a portent? "I would with you, Michel ... yes, I would."

He takes hold of both her hands: "Then let's make it our dream ... I don't know what you're thinking right now, but I too felt something intense a moment ago. And I can feel it again now, a powerful force between us ... I think they call it love, Jeanne." She can't control her tears, her joy. "Yes, I know. I feel it too. I do. I do." He holds her long and close. Her arms are wrapped around him.

"Michel, this is awful. Especially now, but I must go, I ..."

He brushes her bottom lip with his finger: "I know you do. I understand." She stands, finds a vanity mirror in her handbag, and looks at her face: "My teary red eyes will be a challenge for the make-up girls at the studio."

"Buy a chilled cucumber from the vendor on the Rue de Rivoli. Tell him I sent you. He owes me."

"You fool!"

"I know. Mad and impetuous, that's me." Her tears dissolve to smiles, she starts to dress. He watches her. "When will I see you next, Jeanne?"

"I don't know. As soon as I can."

He's very aware that time is running out. He gets up and finds Camille's pink shop pinafore, puts his head through the loop and wraps it around himself, lacing it at the front. It's much too small and it looks crazy on him, and she cannot suppress a laugh. "I'll see you out," he says seriously, securing the knot.

"Dressed like that? I don't think so."

"Why not, we are in the Marais."

"Where are you staying?"

"The Hôtel du Petit Moulin, It's right across the street. They had one room left." That's it, she's back in her white silk dress. He moves nearer to her, takes her hand: "Tomorrow?"

Jeanne hesitates a moment: "Yes, tomorrow. Although I can't think how or where at the moment." She withdraws from their closeness and starts to leave: "I won't forget our dream, Michel. I promise." She pauses: "But really, you can't come down into the shop dressed like that. Someone might look in the window and see you. Think of Camille's reputation."

"Alright, if you say so."

"I'll call you at your hotel later."

She closes the door and Michel hears her cautiously descending the stairs into the shop, then the ting of the bell as the door closes. He leans back against the wall and scrunches his yes shut: I've just told her I love her, which I do. There is no turning back now ... the journey has started ...

Michel returns to the bed settee, opens Jeanne's Evian, and finishes it off; a million thoughts running through his mind. A solitary bleep suddenly resonates in the silent room, breaking his reverie. He stands, takes his mobile from out of his jacket pocket. Caller/Message ID: Noah Gagnon at Piermaster Corporation, Canada.

Gagnon is straight in as normal: "Toujours à Paris, Mike?"

("Are you still in Paris, Mike?")

"Oui."

("Yes.")

"Ça avance?"

("Any progress?")

"Un peu, oui."

("Some, yes.")

"Il y avait une vente, à Londres. Une seule bouteiile de Cognac Massougnes 1802 s'est   vendue pour deux cent cinquante mille livres. Imaginez un peu la valeur du magot des Nazis."

("There was an auction in London. A single bottle of
Cognac Massougnes 1802 made two hundred and
fifty thousand pounds. Imagine what the Nazi haul
is worth.")

"Impossible."

("I can't.")

"Tenez-moi au courant."

("Keep me posted.")

The line goes abruptly dead; Michel says to himself: Why am I doing this? The man is a tyrant. He gathers his things together and removes Camille's pink pinafore with a trace of a smile. All he can think of is Jeanne and what he said to her.

*

Michel leaves the shop and walks down the Rue du Poitou. Then he hears a sound. He turns; nothing; waits. He continues, slightly increasing his pace, a little wary now. There it is again. A sound, a movement. Behind, the sound of slightly faltering footsteps. The clandestine rhythm of pursuit: a tail. Michel quickens his pace, continually looking over his shoulder for a sign of his pursuer. His gait is between a walk and a run. Fortunately, it's quiet at this time of the evening. Twenty minutes of cat-and-mouse and then finally, confident he has lost the tail, he finds a random nightclub and walks straight up to the bar counter to order a drink. He's in such a hurry that he fails to notice the motif of a pink moustache over the door. And a predominantly male clientele. The barman finally comes over to serve him.

"Ricard, s'il vous plait." Michel thinks of his father and tries to sound as Parisian as possible. Someone might ask the barman at a later date.

You never know.

Hôtel du Petit Moulin

Rue du Poitou, Paris

MICHEL HAD DRUNK ENOUGH Ricard to quell his nerves, after the chase. But his banter was sufficiently coherent to persuade Eric, the proprietor of the Pink Moustache, that he lived near la Gare du Nord. He worked for SNCF – as a train manager - and had met a lovely English tourist called Jane. He'd had an amorous afternoon with her in a hotel in the Marais. Now he needed a few drinks to recover from his ardent exertions.

Eric was amused by his raunchy story. Later that evening, he returns to his hotel room and collapses on top of the double bed. There are clothes spread all over the carpet. Michel lies naked on top of a duvet, face down in the darkened room. The radio alarm reads: 23:36. A bottle of water stands by. The landline telephone beside him buzzes and buzzes and buzzes. Finally, he stirs, pokes out his arm, and finds the receiver.

Jeanne whispers softly: "Michel?"

He fumbles for the water, unable to speak, badly dehydrated from mixing alcohol. "Michel?"

"Yes, yes, I think so." He grabs the bottle of Evian and slurps water clumsily; it dribbles down his chin.

"You sound odd."

"I was sound asleep 40 seconds ago."

She raises her voice a notch: "I've tried your room loads of times."

"I was out."

"Clearly ... I just wanted to say goodnight."

Michel rallies: "Goodnight ... Oh, I saw you on T.V. With Fieschi."

"On the TV in your room?"

"No. I was in a bar, actually."

"Oh, a bar. Yes, I see ... Fieschi needed to be there. He's the producer. I told you." Careful; don't sound possessive: "Is he always with you on such occasions?" He asks her warily.

"Yes, he's the main financier ... Are you alright? You sound odd." There is a long awkward moment: "I had the feeling that I was being followed tonight, after I let myself out of the shop."

"And were you?"

"Yes. I managed to lose them. That's how I ended up in the Pink Moustache nightclub in the Marais. It was quite an experience. All perfectly innocent, of course."

Jeanne laughs: "I'm pleased about that, Michel."

"Will I see you tomorrow?" He tries not to sound too needy, but his hangover has already begun in earnest.

"Yes, somehow, Michel. Somehow."

"Sweet dreams, Jeanne."

"And you too." The phone clicks off and he stares up at the ceiling, his mouth tacky, mind full of thoughts. How much he wanted to say three simple words.

Rue du Poitou

Confiserie Boissier, Paris

MICHEL IS SUFFERING BADLY. It's now the following morning and he sits in the hotel's breakfast room drinking black coffee and eating scrambled eggs with French bread. He's already rehydrated himself with grapefruit juice and Evian. But it's not just the result of mixing cheap red plonk with too many Ricards. His malaise is two-fold: he knows he was pursued the previous night, and he is sure it relates somehow to Fieschi. The second is Jeanne and her predicament – I am married, Michel – those fateful words she uttered at Aunt Bénédicte's house only forty-eight hours previously. And now they'd shared an evening of passion, but what did it all mean? Was he fooling himself? How could they possibly be together with a man like Fieschi breathing down their necks?

After his petit déjeuner he feels vaguely human again. He dashes across the street, dodging traffic, to Camille's shop. It is fortunate for him she doesn't open her doors until 10.00 am –

'*who on earth buys bonbons at 8.00 am?*' – he's heard Jeanne say at some point. He opens the door and Camille looks up at him:

"Ah, you are returning my key, good. Don't worry, I washed up your dirty glass and threw away the empty wine bottle. I must say I'd have thought you'd had more taste than to buy a four-Euro bottle of plonk."

Her mood disarms him: "Good morning, Camille."

"Good morning, Michel." She holds out her hand for the key and raises her eyebrows expectantly.

"It's back at my hotel."

"Oh, you have a hotel, do you? I assumed you'd kipped on my sofa bed, given the state of the place this morning." She labours the point further. "The sheet is in with the laundry, by the way ... so there's no need for you worry about it."

He tries not to look too sheepish and angles his head across Rue du Poitou: "Yes. I'm staying at the hotel opposite ... Le Petit Moulin ... quite comfortable." "Oh, so no expense spared then. What an old romantic you really must be." She finally smiles. "Bring it in later, I don't need it now. Your evening was consummate, so I hear? The deed was done, and she didn't even ask for her money back?"

"Camille, really."

"Camille, really." She impersonates his Canadian accent wickedly. "Sorry. I can't resist joshing with you because you look so sheepish and well, vulnerable. Is it guilt? The morning after the night before ..."

"I happen to be suffering from a rather nasty hangover."

"Poor you, Michel." At that moment a lady comes into the shop and dithers forever before purchasing two pieces of Turkish Delight. "Sorry, I'm being beastly to you. Tell me all ... not your liaison amoureuse with Jeanne. Everything else."

Michel explains how he was followed – by persons unknown – and had accidentally ended up in the Pink Moustache, drinking Ricard.

"Your pursuer wasn't just a random coincidence then? I mean, you're not just imagining you were being followed?"

He takes a breath of frustration: "No, Camille. I am not imagining it."

"Good. Did your pursuer see you leave here?"

Michel thinks for a moment: "No, I don't think so."

"He or she must have commenced their pursuit from somewhere. Where was it?" "I have no way of knowing that do I? How could I?"

"You wouldn't make a very good spy, would you? Sneaking through the streets of Paris with the bad guys on your tail?"

"No, I suppose not." He pauses for a moment; because he needs to up his game: "What is it, Camille? What hold does Fieschi have over Jeanne?"

She stands there silent and motionless. And surprised at the unexpected directness of the question.

"What hold, Camille? Why is Jeanne married to Fieschi? What's the reason?" "Haven't you asked her?"

"I wanted to ask you first."

"Not a very convincing answer." She looks at him cautiously. "Because she loves him, what other reason could there be?"

It's clear that Camille doesn't want to discuss the matter further; he is prying into their personal family affairs, and he has no right. She takes a deep breath and looks him in the eye: "Just go away, please. Leave us alone. You are trouble. We were managing perfectly well before you came onto the scene."

"She crashed into my car. I didn't come onto the scene. It was happenstance."

Camille stares at him blankly: "Oh, yes, she told me about that ... was there much damage?" Her tone borders on sarcasm.

He moves closer to the glass cabinet full of confectionery careful not to lean on it: "Can't we at least be friends, Camille?"

She plucks a pair of glasses out of the pocket of her pink pinafore and puts them on, as if wanting to see him more clearly: "Why? Why should we be?"

"Do you want to talk? Can I help?"

"There is nothing in the world I would want to talk to you about, if I am honest." "You paint a very dismal picture, Camille."

"I paint a very real picture, Michel, to use your vernacular. You are a man with whom my sister has unwisely fallen in love ..."

He brightens at the sound of that single word: "She said that?"

"Don't fish, it doesn't suit you ... The romance is doomed, so forget it. Walk away. Walk away from the château, walk away from us."

"Because of Fieschi, you mean?"

She takes off her glasses, polishes them with her pinafore: "Because it makes sense. Now please leave. I have a business to run ... post the key in through the letterbox later. When I have gone home."

Michel realizes he's on a hiding to nothing: "OK." He turns and leaves the shop, looking left and right across Rue du Poitou.

Inside, Camille takes out her mobile, punches a number from her contacts. Then, thinking better of it, cancels the call.

*

Another tail, across the road, Marcel, attempts to merge with the crowd. His earpiece and wire are a dead giveaway. He searches desperately for Michel but can't see him. Suddenly he spots him up ahead and he's walking fast. Marcel follows him, keeping a cautious distance between them. Michel walks on, appears oblivious.

Despite Camille's disingenuous comments about his espionage skills, Michel is suddenly aware he's being followed again. He stops and looks into a shop window searching for a reflected image of a pursuer; he'd seen it in an old spy movie. He's checking, calculating, watching; every sinew of his body alive and wary: could the man be armed? Did he intend to kill him?

Marcel stops. The trail continues, cat-and-mouse, cat-and-mouse. Michel ducks into a street café. The tables and chairs outside it are crowded with customers, drinking coffee and people-watching. He hastily orders an espresso from a waiter at the counter. He takes out his mobile and consults the bill from the Hostellerie de la Poste at Lignières. He dials.

Meanwhile, somewhere out on the street, Marcel doesn't know what to do, he's lost his quarry. He waits around, hoping to spot him.

The Hostellerie landline is answered after three rings: "Marie-Christine? Good morning to you. It's Michel ... thank you so much ... ah, you have spoken to Jeanne today ... yes, the trouble is I've lost her again. No, Camille was very helpful. Any ideas where Jeanne might be today? Where did she call you from?"

The waiter serves his espresso which Michel drinks in two gulps. He leaves a five Euro note under the saucer and resumes his conversation with Marie-Christine: "Sorry. I have no idea where Exposure Photographique is located. Never heard of it. But please, just text me the address and code postal; I'll find it. Thank you ... appreciated, really."

He cancels the call and quickly walks out of the café, still looking left and right. His vigilance is undiminished as he dashes back to Rue du Poitou ...

*

Michel returns to his hotel room, takes out his laptop and goes on the internet. Google search:

`Jeanne Rey, film star + Cannes Film Festival.`

Newspaper pages immediately flash up: Le Monde – Le Figaro – Libération – Les Echos. He scrolls back to Le Parisien: more or less the same page he saw on the train showing Jeanne's face at Cannes. Sud Ouest, Bordeaux – similar – but more focus on the 'local- girl made-good' angle. How she was chosen to play the part of Isabelle Loiseau out of 250 applicants in an audition. Jeanne's new film was shot mainly on location in England. He reads the story; it's interesting but it's not the information he's really looking for. He types an enquiry into the browser once again:

`Fire at Château Boissier 15 juin 2018, Poitou-Charentes.`

And hits the search bar. The result is immediate:

Incendie au château Boissier ... incendie ravage château, deux victimes.

He presses 'translate' out of curiosity:

Fire devastates château Boissier ... two die.

Michel scrolls down the article.

Twin sisters Camille and Jeanne Boissier escaped death

114

yesterday, thanks to the bravery of passer-by Carlo Fieschi, the famous Corsican film producer. Their parents, Gérard and Edith, were not so fortunate.

There are numerous photos of the devastated château and rows of Cognac vines. Michel scrolls down to a later date and finds further features:

Hero Carlo Fieschi to act as legal guardian of fire tragedy twins.

Yet more photos and features:

Fire tragedy twins: an exclusive interview with detective Gaston Leclerc, Commissariat de Police Cognac.

Local public notary Serge Antonelli to oversee Boissier estate for fire tragedy twins Camille and Jeanne.

Michel whistles to himself: "Antonelli ... yes. Now that's a name I know." He clicks to more links and searches one last time:

Jeanne Rey + marriage + family.

Again the result is quick:

Fire survivor to wed her rescuer, Carlo Fieschi. Photos of the couple, Pascal and Marie-Christine, Camille, and Aunt Bénédicte. Witness: Serge Antonelli.

Just as Michel logs off, he receives the expected text message from Marie-Christine. He looks at the address:

Exposure Photographique, Avenue Kléber, 75116 Paris. Rear
courtyard entrance door. M-C.

He takes a swig from his bottle of water, briefly straightens the ruffled duvet, and leaves the room, locking the door behind him.

Outside the hotel, he turns and walks quickly east to St. Lazare railway station. Marcel is trailing behind, struggling to keep up. Cat-and-mouse once again; the game is on.

Gare St. Lazare, Paris

Ticket Office

MICHEL BUYS A TICKET using his Visa card. He walks away and glances up at the SNCF Departures display board: Le Havre, Cherbourg, Caen. He has seen Marcel three times during *his coup de théâtre*. Once outside the Petit Moulin – across the street – and twice in the railway station.

He checks his watch, then his ticket and dashes over to platform 8. Marcel does the same. Michel boards the train and runs down through five carriages and then quietly gets off at the other end, walking onto the platform busy with other passengers. He hides behind a pillar and watches Marcel inside the train anxiously walking up and down the aisle as the doors close for departure. Perfect timing. Michel can see he is desperately searching for him as the train pulls out of the station. Marcel clutches his phone, ready to report to his employer.

Fieschi won't be happy to hear he's lost his quarry, again.

*

Michel leaves the station and runs fast towards the Arc de Triomphe and finds Avenue Kléber. He checks his watch: 14.28.

He smiles to himself: he must remember to tell Camille he's not an incompetent spy after all. Despite everything, he's thoroughly enjoying himself: a beautiful girl; a chase across Paris. And, best of all, his hangover has vanished. So has Marcel. What could go wrong?

Exposure

Avenue Kléber, Paris

AVENUE KLÉBER IS IN THE 16th arrondissement of Paris in the Chaillot quarter. It is one of twelve avenues that converge on Place Charles de Gaulle. Exposure Photographique is in one of the grand old buildings designed by Haussmann.

Stéphane, another of Fieschi's men, pursues Jeanne down the winding staircase outside to a scruffy rear courtyard where the photographers sit and smoke during breaks. He finds her sitting on a wooden bench, clutching a handkerchief, crying.

He approaches her cautiously: "What's wrong, Miss Rey?"

"My sister has been taken to hospital."

"Her arm?"

Jeanne shakes her head, the tears streaming: "No, not her arm. Worse." She's hysterical, he moves closer to her, concerned: "Then, what? An accident?" More tears, more drama. She clasps hold of his arm: "No, it's worse than that, Stéphane. Much worse.

Psychiatric ward. Breakdown. I must go to her. Please don't tell Mr. Fieschi. He just won't understand. Not a word, I beg you."

She hands him a large bundle of Euros, which he takes: "This will help cover any unforeseen expenses." She doesn't say like the termination of your employment. But it might be understood. Fieschi's staff come and go with alarming regularity. Stéphane nods his head with an air of embarrassment, then he leaves.

Once he's safely out of sight, she pulls out her mobile: "Camille! Please close the shop quickly. Now! Meet me at the Georges Cinq in two hours or so. You may have to kill time in a department store. I need you to act as my alibi ... I'm sure you can guess why. See you later, in the lounge. Thanks!" She doesn't give her sister the opportunity to question her or even to refuse.

Jeanne frowns: she feels bad about using Camille so unashamedly. But hoodwinking Stéphane was easy. After all, she is an actress. She walks out towards the rear courtyard entrance door she had explained to Marie-Christine.

*

Michel finds the door, opens it and there she is. She runs towards him, wraps her arms around him.

"Are you ok?" he asks.

She says: "I am now. But we need to leave. I've booked a suite at the Georges Cinq Hôtel. I took the precaution of using your name. Hope that's alright? I dare not use my own." "Sure."

"Camille's meeting me there later ... I had to use her as my alibi in case Fieschi or one of his men starts asking questions about where I am. He's always on my case. Day and night." "Hmm ... I'm not sure that I'm Camille's favourite person."

"First impressions don't always count, Michel."

"No, but this was my second."

"Ha! You ask too many questions ... I could probably have answered most of them. I told you I would."

"Yes, I know. But being followed by one of Fieschi's thugs made me nervous." "I'll make it up to you. Promise."

Hôtel Georges Cinq

Av. George V, 75008, Paris

THE ART DECO SUITE is sumptuous; and, had the curtains been open, they could have seen the Arc de Triomphe at the top of the Champs-Élysées. But time is of the essence; Michel and Jeanne are in bed in the darkened bedroom; an ice bucket stands beside it.

"You told this Stéphane your sister had had a breakdown? She'll be furious if she ever finds out."

"She won't."

"At least it worked. Come here, you beautiful girl." He kisses her passionately and, once again, their desire is overwhelming. Suddenly Michel's mobile on the bedside cabinet vibrates. He curses: "Not now."

She pulls away: "Aren't you going to answer it?"

"No, this is more fun."

"It could be important." She sits up in the bed.

The phone persists, then stops, then rings again.

"Ah, not now," he says again impatiently.

"Then I will ... it could be Camille."

"I doubt it. She doesn't have my..." Before he can stop her, she leans across, grabs the iPhone, and looks at the screen: Face Time app: Noah Gagnon of Piermaster Corporation, Canada.

He's straight in, his usual hard-edged tone.

"Mike? Enfin, qu'est-ce qui se passe? Où-êtes vous donc sapristi?"

("Mike? What's going on? Where the hell are you?")

Gagnon sees Jeanne's face on screen. Michel grabs the phone. Jeanne is confused; she sits up. Michel attempts bright and breezy and sits up in bed a little straighter.

"Noah! Quelle bonne surprise! Je ..."

("Noah! How lovely to hear from you. I ...")

"Laissez tomber les conneries! Bondieu, où êtes-vous donc?"

("Cut the crap. Where are you?")

"Ah, - à Paris."

("Ah, - Paris.")

"Toujours à Paris? C'est en Charentes que vous devriez vous trouver. Pas à Paris! Alors, avez-vous enfin pu vous renseigner sur les propriétaires du château? Votre piste, elle vous a mené quelque part?"

123

("Paris, still? Did you find out who owns the château? That's what you said you were doing. Any leads?")

Jeanne swings her legs out of the bed, concerned, and asks him what's going on?

"Qu'est ce que qui se passe, Michel? Quoi?"

He shakes his head, implying 'not now'. She can't hide her growing fear as Michel continues his conversation with the mysterious Noah.

"Oui, oui, je m'occupe de l'affaire ..."

("Yes, yes, I'm on the case ...")

But Noah Gagnon is not to be placated. He can see on his screen at the other end of the line in Canada that Michel's in bed with a beautiful woman; and his sexual indiscretion is on the firm's time. He raises his voice to be sure the whole of France can hear his utter indignation:

"Vous n'en avez pas l'air! L'affaire est en Charente. Du Cognac Nazi caché sous un moulin à vent. Pas à Paris dans une chambre d'hôtel avec une pute ... Mais qu'est-ce que vous pouvez bien foutre? Vous avez des explications?"

("No you are not! The business in hand is in the Charente. Nazi Cognac hidden under a windmill. Not in a Paris hotel bedroom with a hooker ... What's going on?")

Jeanne snatches the iPhone from Michel and looks directly at the face of Noah Gagnon. Neither Noah nor Jeanne can comprehend exactly who they are seeing; or why - it doesn't make sense to either of them.

"Il vous rappellera ..." Jeanne says to Noah with undisguised confusion and anger at such an insult. *"He'll call you back ..."* Her words resonate with emotion. She terminates the call, turns to Michel: "And I'll ask you the same question. What's going on? How dare he call me a hooker? Just who the hell does he think he is?" She is fighting tears; but sheer annoyance is getting the better of her.

Michel is completely caught out. He taps the bed sheet where she'd lain not long ago with a come back expression. She ignores it.

She's trembling with emotion: "So, you came to France to find Nazi Cognac? Any more lies? Any more little details you omitted to tell me?"

He sits up.

She's full of hurt: "I told you people let me down and you promised – absolutely – not to be one of those people. Remember?"

He's frozen with guilt. Speechless as she bleeds.

"But you are one of those people, Michel. You are ... you're a liar." He says nothing because he can't.

Her eyes dance with fire and fury: "I really believed in you. I

125

thought – at last – somebody really cares for me ..."

He tries to speak but still can't find the words.

"You've deceived me ... you let me down. Why?" She stops and tries to figure something out. "Our meeting wasn't chance, was it? You knew I'd be there that day. There was no magic – the whole thing was contrived, and I fell for it."

Michel leaps out of bed, goes to his pile of discarded clothes, and pulls on his boxer shorts. He knows their love is over and turns to face her:

"That is not true, Jeanne. And you know it. In your heart you know it." His breathing is fast.

"No, I don't, Michel. Why were you really at Segonzac?"

She walks over to where he is standing, half naked, a metre away from him. Before he can form an answer, she continues:

"Not to buy Château Boissier, was it? As you told me ... as you led me to believe that whole afternoon and evening we were together at Pascal's ..." She finally breaks down in tears and he wants to hold her.

"Partly, yes," he says lamely.

"Partly, yes. What kind of a stupid answer is that? Either you were or you weren't. Which is it? Make your mind up."

"Jeanne, listen ..."

"Which?"

"Please just listen ... I work for – Noah Gagnon – the guy on the

126

phone. He owns Piermaster. They buy and sell rare wine. And Cognac."

Jeanne folds her arms: "So?"

"I was instructed to find 600 old bottles of missing Cognac. 1770 Massougnes. Very rare, very valuable, for a wealthy Japanese buyer. My mission was to find the Cognac and buy it from the owner."

She frowns: "To steal it, you mean?"

"No. To find it and buy it. That was my job and why I was there."

"Nazi Cognac?"

"No! French Cognac."

Jeanne waits, absorbing the facts: "Nazi Cognac is what your friend Noah just said. I heard him. You heard him."

Michel remains quiet, because that is precisely why he couldn't admit to her the real reason for his mission to France.

She narrows her eyes.

He thinks: She can still look beautiful even when she's angry.

Jeanne sighs, persisting: "Yes. So, it must be stolen or looted. Hidden by the French from the Nazis ... And you plan to find it and sell it? However you try and twist it, that's the bottom line."

He nods.

"And you believe it's somewhere on our estate? Yes? That's why you were there. Not to buy, not to restore. It was all lies."

"No, Château Boissier was one of several options because of its age and location. There is also a windmill somewhere which I haven't had time to find."

She's listening but she's still bubbling with hurt.

"It's your choice whether you believe me or not. But when I saw the château I fell in love with it ... and when I met its owner, I fell in love with her too. That's the truth." Suddenly Jeanne gathers her clothes together and starts to dress: "I will never trust you again, Michel. You've let me down." Her voice is quieter now; she has decided. Michel pleads with her: "Jeanne, please?"

"Please what? I've spent four years living with a man I detest. And now you come into it and lie to me. What is it about me that makes people want to deceive me?" "Look, Jeanne. I owe the Canadian tax authorities seventy thousand bucks. It was a chance to pay it off and get my life back." She's seething, not listening. "... and how was I to know I'd meet you?"

She's adamant as she puts the last of her clothes on and retrieves her things from around the hotel suite: "You could have told me the truth and I'd have given you the money. But you chose to lie to me instead."

She's dressed; she walks towards the door.

"I'm sorry ... I ..."

"Don't, Michel. Our dream is dead ..." She pauses, "and don't worry about paying for the suite. If you're so hard up, I'll pay for it myself. And tell him, I am not a whore. I have never been so insulted in my life."

She slams the door. And she's gone.

*

Michel is suddenly exhausted. He walks into the lounge of the sumptuous suite; and opens the long silk drapes with the tug of a cord. Sunlight immediately streams into the room; so bright he has to cover his eyes. Wearily he sits on the sofa to collect his thoughts: what should he do next?

A moment later his phone vibrates again. He goes over and cautiously picks it up and glances at the caller display: 0033 545 ... A French number with an area code for the Charente: maybe it's Camille wanting to make amends?

Michel answers.

"Monsieur Michel Bouchard? This is Serge Antonelli."

"Oh yes, hello."

Antonelli clears his throat: "The vendor of Château Boissier no longer wishes to sell. And he is also prohibiting all access to it, from now on."

"He? I see ... Did he say why?"

"No. I am merely communicating his instruction to me. I am sure the property agent has others in the area."

"What if I were to make a firm offer, higher than the asking price?" "That is up to you," says Antonelli. "But the situation will remain the same, I'm sure." The line goes dead. Michel says to himself: "Great. I've lost Jeanne and now the château too. Tremendous." He puts his head in his hands in despair. "Now, let's just think about this."

Michel pours himself a glass of champagne from the ice bucket and swigs it down in one go. He goes over to his jacket and retrieves a few pages he'd had printed out at the Petit Moulin earlier; the result of his internet search. He looks at one newspaper article and the name he had underlined: Gaston Leclerc, Cognac police.

Commissariat De Police

Rue Richard, 16100, Cognac

MICHEL HAD WALKED WARILY to the front desk at the Georges V to return his room key card. The receptionist told him that the bill had indeed been settled in full, including the bottle of champagne. He's wracked with guilt about everything.

He then returned to the Petit Moulin, gathered his belongings and checked out. The return journey on the TGV had been just as agreeable as the outward. His phone call to the police detective had initially been met with suspicion, but when he mentioned Jeanne Rey, the situation changed.

Now, Gaston Leclerc eyes Michel cautiously, his printouts and newspaper copies cover the desk: "Let me see now, Monsieur Bouchard. French Canadian? Toronto?"

"Quebec. Is my accent that obvious?"

"It is to a humble cop in the wilds of the Charente!" Gaston makes this comment in English in an intonation he'd heard in

American movies on TV.

"Touché!" Michel says in exaggerated French. "I'd like to ask you about château Boissier, please?"

"What of it?"

"I am planning to buy it, or at least, I was."

Gaston is dismissive: "And I am an investigator, not a property agent." "You were the senior officer at the time of the tragic fire." Michel points to a printed page of an article in the Sud-Ouest news and reads out loud: "Fire tragedy twins: an interview with detective Gaston Leclerc."

Gaston doesn't need to look at the article: "So?"

"What happened?"

"Didn't you read all these articles you have gone to the trouble of seeking out and then printing? You had ample time on the train from Paris."

"Did I say I'd come from Paris?"

"No, but there is a return ticket here amongst your things." He points at the SNCF ticket. Michel thinks better of saying touché again and Gaston picks up: "It was a tragic fire and well reported as you have very ably demonstrated with your research, monsieur." Gaston casts his hand over the collection of papers.

Michel: "Two people were killed. You must have formed an opinion?" Gaston studies Michel: "You have more than just a passing interest in the château. Is that not so? Your mention of

132

Jeanne Rey sparked my interest, of course. She is a celebrity in this area. We are proud of the girl from Segonzac whose name is on the Hollywood Walk of Fame. I have been there, and I have a photo to prove it. So?"

Michel knows he must come clean: "I care deeply about her. And I know there are questions unanswered. You must feel that too, or you wouldn't have agreed to see me." Gaston takes a while to respond. How did this Canadian outsider come to be involved romantically with 'his' precious Jeanne? He felt very paternal towards her. Everybody loved her because she was so genuine and unscarred by the American movie business. "Jeanne Rey – née Boissier - is married to the man who saved the girls' lives. A hero. I would tread very carefully if I were you. Fieschi is a rich and powerful film producer. Well connected and influential."

"Advice noted."

"Ah yes, but will it be heeded?"

Michel looks awkward. Gaston continues to hold his stare. He deliberates a few long moments, makes a decision. Finally, he goes over to a filing cabinet, locates a cardboard folder containing a small plastic bag. Inside it is an identity bracelet, MEDIC-ALERT: "I found this outside the front door of the château the night of the fire." He hands the little bag over to Michel who reads: "Gérard Boissier Group AB negative."

"The rarest blood group," Gaston assures him. Michel studies it then hands it back a little confused.

"Found outside, you say?"

Gaston nods, still watching Michel's reactions. He stands decisively, walks to the window, his back turned: "People with such a rare blood group never part with their Medic Alert identity. It's their lifeline."

Michel cuts in: "You never told the girls? Or anyone else?"

Gaston turns, ignoring his question: "What was the question you came here to ask me, Monsieur Bouchard?"

"How did the fire start? There is no mention of cause in any of these articles. And yet, there must have been a cause. Was there an investigation by the pompiers?" Then Gaston delivers a bombshell: "The only conclusion is that Gérard started it himself to kill them all."

Michel's face dissolves into an expression of horror: "Gérard? But why?"

"That we will never know. But for some reason he lost the bracelet outside before he set fire to the château inside. The only explanation – to me – is suicide. Like leaving a note." Michel stands, his face ashen.

Gaston's tone is grave: "I looked at that young girl's face in the hospital, and it broke my heart. I have a disabled child. I took a decision, Monsieur Bouchard. Sometimes a minor detail is best left unmentioned. It would only cause further pain for the two girls. And they'd already had enough."

Michel nods.

"Not strictly procedural. But I can see from your expression, you'd have done the same." "Yes," agrees Michel, "I'm sure I would." He stands and heads for the door. Gaston looks suddenly exhausted, but says anyway: "Remember, my door is open. But please try not to stir up a hornets' nest."

"I wouldn't dream of it. Good day, Inspector Leclerc."

Antonelli

Place du Marché, Lignières-Sonneville, Charente

MICHEL IS WALKING IN the shaded market square. A man is walking a dog across the square, to a quiet small road. Michel sees a brass plaque on the door of a medium size property: SERGE ANTONELLI. NOTAIRE. The man with the dog is obviously aware of Michel following him and speeds up. Michel catches up with him.

"Morning. It's Mr. Antonelli, isn't it? Wait a moment if you please?" Antonelli stops and turns: "What if I don't have time, Monsieur Bouchard?" "I can't make you, of course. But I'd like to know why the real owner of the château has suddenly decided not to sell ... and has restricted access. It's rather sudden, is it not?" "I can't do that. Client/lawyer privilege. I cannot disclose anything without my client's permission. You should know that."

"Tell him or her I will double my offer."

"Hmm, you haven't made one."

"Then I'll make one. Double the asking price."

"Double?"

"Yes."

"But you don't know the asking price – it's on application only. And you haven't applied. So, the answer is no."

Michel pretends not to have heard Antonelli: "That's right, double. Providing I get the vineyards too. Thousands of hectares of Ugni Blanc. I'm told they are best when they are old. Jeanne told me. You know Jeanne, don't you, Mr. Antonelli? She's the owner."

Antonelli looks uncomfortable: "Vaguely. But that's not possible."

"Why not?"

"I've already explained the nature of privilege. Now, if you don't mind ..." Suddenly Antonelli breaks into a trot, nearly tripping over the dog lead. Michel looks down the deserted road and runs after him.

Michel is buzzed with adrenalin and sees Antonelli has now returned to his office and is lurking by the door with a key; he's still with the dog. Michel runs over to him and picks up the dainty-looking French poodle, all pink bows and fluff. He strokes it. Antonelli can't speak, he is paralyzed with fear.

"Cute. Name?" asks Michel.

Antonelli can hardly get the words out: "Don't hurt her."

"Can't hear you, Mr. Antonelli."

"Loulou."

"I'm not a violent man, Antonelli. But the way I feel now ...plus, I am in a great deal of trouble. D'you get it?"

Michel strokes the dog, Antonelli is sick with fear as he continues: "So why don't you just show me the Boissier file ... or I might be forced to cause some damage ... Do you get it?"

The dog yelps as if understanding the implication.

"Now would be the very best time, Antonelli. Sorry to be over-dramatic, but this has not been the best day, believe me."

Antonelli caves in: "Okay, okay. Give me my Loulou." Antonelli grabs the dog and smothers it with sickening kisses. The dog licks his mouth and lips and the sight disgusts Michel.

"Yuk ...but finally we get there."

"Fieschi will kill me."

"If he doesn't I ... now let's go inside, shall we?"

*

The office is like something out of the nineteen fifties: old furniture, but new technology. Computer, keyboard, and phone chargers. Antonelli still clutches Loulou like a baby. "Can I call you Serge, Serge?"

"No. I am known as Mr. Antonelli ... to everyone ... and that includes you." "You married, Serge?"

"No."

"Partner? Parents? Brothers? Sisters?"

"No."

"Good. Now show me the Boissier file." Antonelli is very, very hesitant. "I'll hold Loulou if you like."

Antonelli is horrified: "No!" He carefully puts the dog into an over-the-top basket filled with rugs and fluffy toys. Two bowls and doggy treats sit beside it; Loulou is clearly indulged by her owner. He opens a locked filing cabinet, pressing the keypad of an electronic digital combination lock, much like a safe: "It's in there, help yourself."

"Take the files out, Serge, you know which is which." Michel is ultra-cautious now. Antonelli selects two cardboard folders, puts them onto the desk. Michel sits down and makes himself comfortable.

The first one is labelled: Edith Boissier Estate/ transfer of ownership to Mr. Carlo Fieschi, legal guardian. Witness: Serge Antonelli.

The second: Title Deeds/Land Registry, Château Boissier, Segonzac, /vineyards. Michel then sees the contract signed by Gérard the night of the chess match. The night of the tragic fire.

Michel is shocked at the words he reads: "What's this?"

Antonelli skulks off to a corner of the office as Michel becomes engrossed with the contract and reads it aloud:

"Because Jeanne is under sixteen, Gérard signed a ten-year contract which gave Fieschi: 'sole permission, liberty and ability to enter, approach and manage her career.' Fieschi paid Gérard twenty thousand Euros for exclusivity ..." Michel pauses to absorb the enormity of such brutal legalese ...

"He sold Jeanne out, betrayed her, for his own personal benefit. God, why would Gérard have done that?"

"Who knows?" Antonelli says quietly.

"Does Jeanne know?"

"Of course not. Carlo saved the lives of Jeanne and Camille. He risked his own to pluck them out of the burning building."

"Why don't I believe that?"

"It is all there to believe, Monsieur Bouchard. The record states what happened in black and white."

"Hm ... very convenient, if you ask me."

Antonelli gives Michel a sickening smile: "Nobody is asking you." Michel reads on: "How did the fire start?" The same question he discussed with Gaston earlier.

Antonelli shrugs, indifferent: "No one knows."

"Or even cares any more, right? Is that what you're saying?"

"It was a long time ago."

"Five years is hardly a lifetime, especially when you have the scars to wake up to every morning, Serge. You don't have to look in the mirror. Camille does."

"Better than being dead."

"You're all heart aren't you, Antonelli. Typical damn lawyer." Michel pauses. "So Fieschi owns Château Boissier. Do the girls know that?"

Antonelli shakes his head: "I think they believe he holds it in trust for them." "But he doesn't. He owns it outright. It's in his name, not theirs?"

"Jeanne is too busy with her films and Camille has the Confiserie. They have more in their lives than some wrecked old building nobody cares about. You see it all over France. Beautiful old, deserted properties at the heart of family disputes."

"This is different, Serge, and you know it. Two people dead and two deceived by a Corsican gangster posing as a hero."

"See it as you wish."

Michel searches into the files. Antonelli moves further back into the room. Michel sees a DO NOT BEND envelope, postmarked Angoulême, France. The address is:

Mr Carlo Fieschi. Suite 3. Hôtel Le Maquis,
Grosseto-Prugna, Corsica.

He quickly takes out his phone and googles the address out of curiosity: 'Grosseto Prugna is a commune in the Corse-du-Sud department of France on the island of Corsica. Known as the home of millionaires and celebrities, the area is famous for elegant

141

restaurants and luxury hotels.'

"Fieschi knows how to live, doesn't he? I bet the girls have no idea this place exists." He shows the screen to Antonelli.

"Neither did I."

"Hmm, really." Michel opens the envelope carefully, cautiously pulling out six prints. The first is a picture of Château Boissier ablaze in the darkness of the Charente. The second, a closer shot, Gérard is in the doorway; his foot appears trapped in a crack in the wooden floorboards. Camille is grabbing hold of Gérard's sleeve. Michel cannot determine whether she is pulling or pushing. Smoke is everywhere.

The third image shows Gérard clutching hold of Camille's ankle – she is falling sideways – into the blaze. He shuffles through the prints again. Once more he can't tell if she is pulling or pushing. The crucial question: which is it?

Michel tilts the envelope and out falls a cellophane packet. Inside it is a CANON MEMORY CARD 256GB / 15 juin 2018. Carlo Fieschi.

In the corner of the office, Antonelli is now perched on the arm of a chair and quietly leans over to a wooden table lamp and wraps his hand around it. The cable is taut. Michel is so absorbed with the photos and memory card that he fails to notice what's happening behind him.

Suddenly, Antonelli is on him. He brings the table lamp down towards Michel's head but misses and catches his shoulder. Michel grimaces in pain, rolls off the chair. The electric cable twangs as the plug is torn out of the socket. Antonelli is on top of Michel, tries to cosh him with the base of the lamp. Michel rolls away and delivers an elbow to Antonelli's jaw. The crack is audible. Antonelli drops the lamp. He's dazed.

Michel stands up, points to a door, swaying slightly: "What's in there?"

"Toilets."

"Go. Go in there." As Antonelli passes him, Michel shouts: "Wait!" He taps down Antonelli's jacket, removes two mobile phones, pushes him into the toilet and locks the door from the outside. He smashes both phones on the desk and runs out of the office.

Tuna

Monoprix Store, Rue de l'Église,
Lignières-Sonneville, Charente

MICHEL CHARGES DOWN THE road to the Monoprix and goes inside. He looks quickly around the shop, buys two rolls of strong duct tape, two tins of tuna and a large bottle of water. He pays without a word and runs back to the office.

*

In less than five minutes Michel is back in Antonelli's office. He opens the toilet door. Antonelli is sitting on the floor, a wad of bloody toilet paper pressed to his mouth. "That wasn't so bad, was it? Out you come ... come on, I haven't got all day, you know." Antonelli staggers out, his eyes wide with fear. Michel points to the desk and the computer.

"Sit and type in your password." Antonelli grips furniture to steady himself and makes his way over to his desk and sits as instructed. He opens his email. Michel finds several emails from

144

Fieschi and presses '*print.*' As the first page pops out and into the tray, he picks it up and reads it out loud:

> "*Serge, please instruct the agent to take Château Boissier off the market. For personal reasons I wish to withdraw. Have no further dealings with Michel Bouchard whom I know has already been there at least once. If either Jeanne or Camille contacts you, which I very much doubt, say nothing at all. C.*"

Antonelli looks shocked. It's all happening so fast. Michel grabs hold of the duct tape and binds Antonelli from his shoulders around the back of a chair like a mummy, right down to his ankles. He is totally immobile. He sees the tins of tuna and looks alarmed: "Loulou doesn't like tuna."

"Believe me, she will, Serge. She will."

Michel then binds his mouth and head to the chair, leaving a space for his nose and eyes only. He goes to the printer, collects the printouts and stacks them with the two cardboard folders, the documents and the cardboard envelope with the photos and memory card. With one of the tins of tuna, he smashes the computer screen and keyboard and rips cables out of their sockets. Michel lifts the dog into the toilet cubicle, fills one of the dog bowls with tuna and the other with water. Locks the door. He scans the office in case he has missed something and picks up the office keys.

Antonelli's angry eyes peer out from the slot of the duct tape.

Michel looks at him: "Today is Saturday; you won't be missed until Monday. By then Fieschi will be finished. And so will you ... oh, don't worry. I'll lock up."

Pascal and Marie-Christine

Hostellerie de la Poste

MICHEL OPENS THE TERRACE garden gate; he's carrying two carboard folders containing the documents from Antonelli's safe. Pascal and Marie-Christine are sitting together on the terrace. They look both surprised and frosty as he enters. "Am I intruding?"

Pascal shrugs, says nothing. Marie-Christine looks disappointed but shakes her head with an inquisitive expression. Michel walks forward to the table, hesitantly, looking at them. "I'm sure you have both spoken to Jeanne and I know she is understandably upset with me. I can't say I blame her – in a way."

Pascal scrutinizes him.

"But I was hired to do a job and part of that job meant absolute confidentiality. I had to sign a contract and locate the old Cognac. Whatever the moral ambiguity of my mission that's what I was instructed to do."

Pascal: "And hidden at Château Boissier?"

"Possibly, Pascal. My brief was not that exact. Supposedly, under or in a windmill on the estate, yes."

"A windmill?" This time Marie-Christine poses the question.

"Yesterday Serge Antonelli called me to inform me in no uncertain terms that the vendor of the château had taken the property off the market."

Michel captures their attention.

"So, I think to myself, why? It's been on the market ever since the fire. No one will buy it, because of the tragic unsolved deaths associated with it. Then I come along, full of enthusiasm and the vendor withdraws. It doesn't make sense."

They're both listening now, intrigued.

"Then I discovered that the owner of the château is a gentleman by the name of Carlo Fieschi. Then, of course, it all made sense."

Pascal laughs smugly, looks at his wife: "Not true, it's held in trust for the girls when they reach twenty-five. Fieschi told me when he and Jeanne got married." He emits a confident little laugh to show how correct he is.

Michel hands across the Antonelli documents.

The first one: Edith Boissier Estate/transfer of ownership to Mr. Carlo Fieschi, legal guardian. Witness: Serge Antonelli.

The second: Title Deeds/Land Registry, Château Boissier/vineyards. Pascal and Marie-Christine read the documents with horror. She says quietly: "There is no mention of Jeanne and Camille or a trust fund?"

"No. Because there isn't one."

Pascal is still not convinced: "I understood that the estate was bankrupt; that there were heavy debts against it."

Michel is dismissive: "Gérard may have had a few gambling debts, yes. But the château and the land must be worth a million Euros, surely, and is not mortgaged. Handed down by Edith's mother. Napoleonic law. Fieschi and Antonelli fabricated the debts so they could steal the château from Jeanne and Camille."

Marie-Christine stands, looks at her husband for support: "We owe you an apology." "No, you don't. It is I who owe you. But one thing is clear. As legal guardian of the twins, Fieschi was easily able to trick them, especially with Antonelli to help him. But there's more. Read this."

Michel hands them the legal contract signed by Gérard to give Fieschi permission to exclusively manage Jeanne's career for ten years. And, because she is under sixteen. Signed with an ink fountain pen, Fieschi's well-known trademark. They're stunned. Pascal's head drops: "Gérard sold Jeanne out to Fieschi for twenty thousand Euros. Is that what this means or am I being stupid?"

Michel taps his arm reassuringly. "Exactly. So, what happened to that money? Did it burn in the fire? D'you know what I think?"

They both look at him; want to know what he thinks.

"I think Fieschi was already in the building that night, not passing by as he swore to the police and was later reported. He paid Gérard the cash and Edith found it. The fire started because of the row which Fieschi caused. Money."

Pascal wants it spelt out: "Then what happened to that money?"

"It's not hard to work out. Fieschi retrieved it and pocketed it when he went back in for the girls. That contract is the hold Fieschi has over Jeanne for definite. And, I have a feeling there might be something else as well. Something else that binds them both to him." Pascal stands up and comes over to Michel, seemingly with the weight of the world on his shoulders: "These documents explain part of the story, but not all of it." Michel, perplexed: "Then what?"

Pascal and Marie-Christine exchange an awkward glance: "You will have to ask the girls; particularly Camille. But these papers will help you. No doubt about it." Pascal hands the documents back to Michel.

"But how? Jeanne hates me ... and as for Camille ... well."

"How do you feel about finding the Nazi Cognac now, Michel?" Marie-Christine asks him solemnly.

He sighs and looks her in the eye: "I don't feel anything about it, Marie-Christine. All I want is to have Jeanne back in my arms again. Tell her that she means more to me than anything." His confession has made him moist-eyed, but he can't help it. Marie-

Christine comes over to Michel and touches his arm affectionately: "It will be alright, Michel. I will call Camille and explain to her what you have revealed thanks to these documents. She will see you and she will tell you the truth. It's what you do with it that matters."

Michel nods. He knows exactly what he must do next.

Message

Apartment on Rue Guénégaud, 75006, Paris

CARLO FIESCHI SITS NAKED behind the desk in his study. His broad-shouldered, muscular physique has turned largely to fat. A wet sheen of hair, post-shower, covers his skin like zoic fur. His eyes flare as he listens to the message:

> *'You have reached the offices of Serge Antonelli, senior notaire, Lignières-Sonneville. I am either on another call or in court. Leave a message after the beep.'*

"You're not on another call, Serge. And you are certainly not in court, or I'd know about it. Call me. I want to know what's happening with Bouchard ..." He was going to mention the incompetence of his other lackeys but thought better of it. He leans back in his leather chair and, hearing the click of a door, shields his manhood: "Snr. Palledri? Is that you?"

Bracelet

Commissariat de Police, Cognac

GASTON LECLERC IS TALKING on the office landline. The conversation is animated, humorous and sounds to be private. Michel knocks, enters, clutching the two carboard folders and the envelope full of photographs.

Gaston: "I will call you back, Stéphanie ... yes, of course ... but you never can tell; isn't that what you always say? Au revoir."

Michel raises his eyebrows: "You did say your door is open."

Gaston shrugs, gestures for the seat: "Did you get a new rental car sorted out?" "No, I haven't even reported the old one yet. Haven't had the time." Gaston shrugs again: "Our trains are so prompt, anyway, who needs a car ... in Paris?" Michel pulls out the photographs – one by one – and carefully places them on the desk like a fan of playing cards: "Remember what you told me about Gérard's bracelet?" Gaston leans forward, captivated by the images: "Of course." He picks up the one crucial shot of Camille and Gérard trapped in the doorway of the burning château and studies it carefully, then meets Michel's gaze:

"One question: Is she pulling or pushing Gérard's arm? What d'you reckon?" Michel's tone is uncharacteristically serious.

Gaston takes out a magnifying glass and studies the shot with more precision, gliding the glass over the image so it blurs in and out of focus. He doesn't look up: "I won't even ask you how you came by this image, Monsieur Bouchard. Or the rest of this lot." He places the photo and glass back on the desk and sifts through the other documents. "The name on the envelope is familiar, but not this address ... Hôtel le Maquis, Grosseto-Pragna ... A Corsican commune, as far as I'm aware. Have you got the memory card on which these images are stored?"

Michel hands it over to Gaston who smiles as he weighs it in his hands: "I'll need perhaps twenty-four hours, Monsieur Bouchard."

Michel shakes his head: "Six. I'll need a definitive answer by seven tonight. And I'll need it in Paris, I'm afraid." He gives Gaston a weak smile of appeal.

Gaston grabs the phone again and punches in a three-digit extension number from memory. "Doctor Chevanne?" He says with a serious tone. "Ah, hello there. It's Inspector Leclerc. Please drop whatever you are doing and get over here right away ..." Gaston looks at Michel. "You can relax, Stéphanie is on her way. And she's the best."

Michel grins: so that's who he was on the phone to when he

arrived: "Inspector Leclerc ... Gaston ... I knew I could rely on you."

Photograph

Confiserie Boissier, Rue du Poitou, Paris

BACK IN PARIS AGAIN, Michel dashes across the street to the familiar Confiserie. He glances up and sees Camille in the upstairs window, looking out for him. She comes down to the shop door, flicks the sign from open to closed and opens it. Her face is expressionless. He steps in without a word and follows her upstairs to the stockroom. Suddenly she turns and puts her arms around him and hugs him. He drops the two carboard folders he had taken from Antonelli's office. Some of the documents spill out onto the floor. After a moment, he gently pulls away from her embrace and looks her in the eye:

"What's this, Camille?"

"I've been horrible to you, Michel. Fierce, judgemental, unsociable."

"You had good reason to be critical. I don't blame you. I wasn't totally honest with your sister, so I deserved ..."

"I had a phone call, Michel. But then, you know I did." They are still in a semi-embrace. "You haven't wasted your time in the Poitou-Charentes, I see." She bends down – with a little difficulty because of her arm – picks up the two folders and assorted documents and hands them to him.

"No, I haven't."

She stands back and is immediately serious; like her sister, her mood can swing in the blink of an eye: "My father Gérard gave me this face and he murdered our mother. I killed him, Michel. That's what this is all about."

"Camille ..."

She shakes her head, not listening: "Fieschi saw me. He even photographed it."

Michel stands there silently absorbing her words. He mulls over their meaning. "That's the hold he has over us. You wanted to know the truth ... and now, you do. That's it."

Michel comprehends: "Fieschi blackmailed both of you ...I assumed it was just Jeanne he had a contractual hold over."

"Contractual? What on earth do you mean, Michel?" Camille grabs the documents from him more harshly than she'd intended and studies them all with rising shock: "How the hell did you get this lot? What is it? I'm confused."

Michel takes a pace toward her, gently touches the side of her poor wounded face and holds his hand there. She looks up at him, vulnerable, alone, injured, bereaved. He knows his tears are not far away. He's welling up and she can see just how deeply moved he is: "I am so sorry, Camille... I..." His tears choke him to silence. "But all the answers are here."

She touches his hand on her face: "Show me ... and I know you are sorry." He struggles not to break down, the emotion is raw and powerful, but he knows he must compose himself: "We need to talk."

"Yes."

"I want you to tell me everything. I'm on your side, Camille."

"I know."

"Both you and Jeanne."

"I know that now, of course I do. I'm sorry about ..."

"There's no need. I'd feel the same if I were you."

Camille takes a deep breath: "Jeanne is speaking at a live television show tonight at Babylon studios. I hope what I tell you won't change anything."

"No, by the time you've read these documents you'll know the truth," Michel says, still moist eyed.

"I've got guest passes for the TV show. D'you think we'll be able to attend?"

*

They walk across the room and sit down on the familiar bed

settee and make themselves comfortable.

"In some ways Genie has been more of a prisoner than I have." She turns her head as if looking into a dark room full of secrets and hidden memories.

Michel nods with a smile which dissolves to quizzical: "Genie?"

"It was a family joke when we were growing up. Jean Genie is a David Bowie song. Aladdin Sane I think was the album. It was Maman's special name for her. Only close family were permitted to call Jeanne Genie. Aunt Bénédicte can get away with it, just. But not even Marie-Christine would overstep the mark."

"Genie, yes, I like that. And I can remember the song, of course."

"I hope you are ready for what I am about to tell you, Michel." Camille bites her lip, suddenly very serious.

"And I hope you are ready to see what's in this lot." He points at the documents he liberated from Antonelli and hopes for the best.

Taxi

Avenue de Clichy, Paris

CAMILLE LOOKS OUT OF the taxi onto the busy avenue. She sees Michel emerge from a gentleman's outfitters wearing evening dress. He checks his bow tie and enacts the 007 stance which makes her laugh. Even the driver makes a comment as Michel gets in and sits beside her. He puts the carrier bag containing his own day clothes down into the footwell.

"I won't say 'Good Evening, Mr. Bond.'" Camille says in excellent English. "I'm impressed, I really am. Anyway, I must look my best when I'm in such wonderful company."

She squeezes his arm: "Flattery won't get you anywhere ... but don't stop trying!" "I won't. And that's a line I've heard before, isn't it?"

She laughs: "Yes. And now, I'm impressed. A misspent youth going to the movies?"

"Just a misspent youth."

The taxi pulls into the night. It's busy: lights, landmarks, people. They look out at Paris by night as the taxi threads through the traffic towards its destination. The radio plays RTL Paris in the background. Michel's phone bleeps and he answers, putting the message on the speaker phone. The husky tones of Noah Gagnon once again.

"Mike. C'est moi, Noah. Pas de résultats, donc plus de contrat. Il ne vous reste plus qu'à trouver quelqu'un d'autre pour payer vos impôts."

> *("Mike. It's me, Noah. You got zero results, so I am terminating our contract. You'll just have to find someone else to pay your tax bill.")*

Gagnon terminates the call abruptly without further ado. Michel switches his phone off and dumps it into the carrier with his belongings. Camille nuzzles her head against his shoulder: "I'd say you've got plenty of results, Michel. Forget about him."

"I will ... whatever will be ... will be."

Babylon

Boulevard Périphérique, Paris

CAMILLE'S AND MICHEL'S TAXI pulls up outside Babylon TV studio on the Périph. They immediately face a barrage of fans, tourists, and paparazzi. The atmosphere is mayhem with people pushing and shoving to get a better view of celebrities of tv, media and sport. Selfies are being taken and there are flashes from the cameras of press photographers.

"My God! Who'd want to be famous if this is the price?" Camille asks him. They get out of the taxi and jostle through the crowds showing their GUEST PASSES to the well-built security men and studio staff.

She covers her hair and face with a silk scarf, so she is not mistaken for her sister.

*

Inside the studio's cinema, on a massive screen, footage from

163

Jeanne Rey's new film is being projected. The audience chatter excitedly.

On the screen:

UN SEUL BILLET starring JEANNE REY

Beside the stage is a panel of four people and the words:

FILM REVIEW. Jeanne, Fieschi (the producer), Raymond (the director), a co-star.

A TV host takes control. The footage stops and house lights brighten. Appreciative applause and cheers from the enthusiastic audience. They are all there to see Jeanne and bathe in the radiance of celebrity.

The host kicks off the evening's events: "So, Jeanne Rey, welcome. It's great to see you; and looking so wonderful ..."

Pause for the audience to spontaneously clap and whistle in appreciation. "Tell us a little about your new movie ... set in England, so we hear."

"Good evening. Thank you ..." A little self-deprecating wave and a smile. She looks every bit the million-dollar star; hair and make-up perfect; figure-hugging haute couture dress and the dazzling smile which captivated Michel in the garden at the château. "I think they're pleased you're here, Jeanne." Another roar of approval. "I play Isabelle, niece of Isambard Kingdom

Brunel, the famous Victorian engineer. His father Marc was French, from Hacqueville, which is partly why I chose to play the role." "What is the genre? Historical fiction?"

"Certainly, costume drama ... a Victorian detective story – very fast moving and great locations too."

The host consults his notes: "Brunel is the man who built railways and ships? But the hero of the film is Harry Brooke, who is fictional?"

"Yes ... I can't give too much away ... and the director Raymond ..." Jeanne points at the panel ... "wanted to create a classic Hitchcock atmosphere ... which I think he did very skillfully. There is plenty of tension and suspense."

"What was it like working on location in England?"

"It was fun. The main cast and some of the crew shared a huge Victorian house in Clifton, Bristol. We got to know each other off-screen. It worked well ..."

The host continues: "And does your character Isabelle have a romance with Harry Brooke? Is there love in the air?"

She laughs warmly: "You'll have to buy a single cinema ticket and see for yourself." Another round of applause in acknowledgment of her play on words.

"That will make Mr. Fieschi very happy," the host says innocently.

It's as if a dark shadow has been cast over her face and her eyes say it all: passion and fury. She tries to conceal it: "I-I hope so, yes."

The host cuts in diplomatically: "Let's show a clip – no spoilers – then we'll take some questions."

The house lights dim, and the screen is full of action. A fierce fight on the Great Western Railway train from London Paddington to Bristol; Harry Brooke is attacked by an assailant ... will he survive?

Camille turns to Michel: "She's as nervous as hell. I've never seen her look so awkward. What can be wrong?"

"I think it was the mention of Mr. Fieschi that pulled the plug."

As the screen images fade and the house lights brighten again, Jeanne is suddenly back to her usual carefree self:

"The cinema needs more stories like this ... action with a heart ..." She turns to her colleagues, to involve them. "Anyway, we are here to answer questions." The host agrees: "Let's open it up. Anyone?"

lady's hand shoots up; she's blushing, a little embarrassed: "Do you keep all the great costumes?"

"No, they all came from the Bristol wardrobe department or were hand-made here in Paris." More laughter and a few claps.

"Did you have to perform any stunts, Miss Rey? As Isabelle?"

"Jeanne, please ... I'm just the girl next door ..." Pause for laughter ... "No. Harry Brooke gets all the fight scenes ... I had to learn how to play the piano!"

More laughter as a lot more hands shoot up; the mood has lightened. Jeanne is now relaxed and in her comfort zone, totally in control.

A hand shoots up: "Your previous film about the orphan from Ukraine was a very human story. Would you say this was in any way similar, Jeanne?"

Michel and Camille who are sitting in the audience turn and around to check where the exit is. And a moment later stand and walk toward it.

*

In the front of house area of the studio, Gaston Leclerc comes in at the eleventh hour clutching his laptop. He is accompanied by Dr. Stéphanie Chevanne, a forensic specialist in her late thirties, whom Gaston summoned to his office yesterday. Gaston smiles at Michel with a mixture of encouragement and mischief. Michel turns to Camille:

"Let's do it."

Camille has no idea what's about to happen, but she takes his hand and kisses it anyway; Gaston is touched at this act of tenderness. He's felt an avuncular sense of responsibility towards the sisters since the fire; and become fond of both.

*

Michel walks down the main aisle of the theatre slowly, his

hand raised to ask a question. Jeanne, still in front of the screen, looks positively shocked. A spotlight picks Michel out. Fieschi looks as angry as hell and turns to the director. A boom mike moves in close to Michel as he makes his way down toward Jeanne and the panel. He's straight in with his own question, directed specifically at Fieschi:

"Yes, we certainly do need a human story, don't we, Mr. Fieschi. And, as a celebrated film producer, I have one for you ... it will sound tantalizingly familiar ..."

The audience wait; nobody's intervening. The host is transfixed; he looks up into the control room; the director nods and smiles: whatever is happening is happening on his watch and he is not going to stop it.

Michel fixes his eyes on Fieschi: "Two guys play chess, in a château, for big money. One loses heavily to the other. Then, supposedly, the other man leaves. A terrible row occurs between the loser, Gérard, and his wife, Edith." He pauses for effect. "What could be the cause of a row that ends in a tragic fire?"

Jeanne's hand shoots up to her mouth in shock; Fieschi looks uncomfortable. The audience are spellbound as Michel waits ten long seconds before answering his own question: "How about twenty thousand Euros ... you happened to be there, Fieschi, didn't you?" Michel's expression is dead pan. You could hear a pin drop in that crowded theatre.

"Yes, you were. In fact, it was you who heroically rescued two young girls – beautiful twins – any ideas? Is there a charred smell of familiarity, Mr. Fieschi?   The host looks up at the director again. He loves every minute of this. He can see the headlines tomorrow: fame and publicity!

Fieschi roars: "I've heard enough of this damn nonsense."

He starts to stand but Raymond courteously prevents him, whispering something in his ear about reputation. It's live TV, Fieschi is in a fix, his credibility goes if he walks. But, he can't stand it and shoots out of his chair shouting: "Stop the cameras ... I demand you stop the cameras!"

But the director up in the control room is desperate to keep the cameras rolling. Michel produces the contract signed by Gérard. He waves it around to provoke Fieschi. Which it does because he knows exactly what the wording is. And what it meant. "Recognise this, Fieschi?"

Fieschi charges over to Michel and makes a clumsy grab: "How the hell did you get this, you damn thieving bastard?"

Jeanne runs over to Michel; she seizes the contract and reads it as fast as she can. Michel continues, his voice raised: "You essentially bought a fifteen-year-old girl for twenty thousand Euros. You were so obsessed with Jeanne that you framed her sister for murder." Jeanne cannot believe her eyes; she is so mortified that she bursts into tears. And she is not acting. Some of the audience turn to their neighbours thinking: is this all part of the presentation?

Somebody shouts call the police. Somebody else replies you must be joking, this is gold! Two theatre security men come from behind the set and grab Fieschi to restrain him. On cue Gaston stands up with Dr. Chevanne, who very hastily sets up a power-point presentation with her laptop. Moments later, projected onto the large cinema screen, the audience are shocked to see:

The photograph of Château Boissier ablaze in the darkness among the acres of vineyards in the Poitou-Charentes.

Next image: Gérard is in the doorway of the building; his foot appears trapped. Camille is grabbing hold of Gérard's hand and forearm; his shirt sleeve is taut. It's impossible to determine if she is pulling or pushing her father. It is obvious she is choking with smoke fumes; and the heat must be intense.

The audience stares at the screen in shock. Fieschi is still being restrained by the security men. Jeanne is speechless, her eyes flicking from the screen to Michel and the audience. Presently, an educated voice fills the room, articulate and clear. Dr. Chevanne is in the shadows, microphone in hand:

"The arm consists of a complex system of muscles and tendons ..." This photograph is zoomed in to magnify the image of Camille's arm. "In this picture we can observe that the triceps muscle is relaxed whereas the biceps muscle is contracted. Judging by the fist balled around the sleeve's material, it's my opinion that Camille was trying to pull the man away from where he was trapped and consequently away from the fire."

Fieschi struggles with futility as Gaston produces the identity bracelet, his ace card and wanders down to the podium:

"I am Inspector Gaston Leclerc of the Commissariat of Police, Cognac. And that was the voice of a forensic specialist on my team ..." He pauses so the audience, Fieschi, Jeanne and the panel can absorb his next words ...

"Camille pulled with such force, to save her father, that she wrenched off his precious bracelet. And he fell backwards into the fire. I found this bracelet."

Doctor Chevanne continues: "Judging by this next image, it is my professional opinion that the burning floor literally swallowed him up. An accident. A tragic accident, but nothing more sinister."

Gaston confronts Fieschi. Jeanne and Michel join him: "And you blackmailed those girls for a murder they did not commit. For five years you had them believe a total lie, Mr. Fieschi. And you took Château Boissier from them. Their mother's heritage. As they say in the world of Cognac, you stole la part des anges – the angels' share."

There is total silence in the theatre apart from Fieschi still struggling with the two security guards. But his fight is done because he knows he's finished. His career is over, and prison awaits.

Suddenly there is a commotion at the back of the studio. Camille marches down the aisle, brushing off the usherettes and continues down towards the stage. Simultaneously, she's struggling to rip off her blouse with her right arm (her left is in a cast), revealing her burns to Fieschi, to the world. The audience watch her every move, transfixed. The cameras follow her as she joins her sister and Michel. She turns to Michel as he slips off his dinner jacket and wraps it around her bare shoulders.

She whispers: "Now Michel, now we can be friends ... Jeanne and I are no longer prisoners. You have freed us both from five years of hell."

The three of them hug, shaking with emotion. You could hear a pin drop in that packed studio. Because every member of the audience feels the same.

Celebrity

Pink Moustache Nightclub, the Marais, Paris

THERE IS NO DOUBT about the identity of the celebrity as the doorman admits her into the busy nightclub. Heads turn, voices are lowered as she walks towards the bar. Eric is about to caution Michel against a third Ricard when she joins Michel at the bar. Everybody knows who Jeanne is, of course, and Eric is gushing with enthusiasm: iced water, club coasters and bar snacks.

"I thought I might find you here, Michel," she says, glancing at Eric. "After your adventures the other evening ..." Eric pouts his lips in mock apology and smooths down his striped apron.

"Jeanne. Thank goodness," says Michel cautiously. "I thought I'd lost you." "I'm afraid you have, Michel. I'm sorry and I'll explain why presently." "Oh?" He is flabbergasted.

Jeanne accepts a chilled Chablis from Eric and lowers her voice: "What you did tonight at the TV studio was extraordinary, unexpected and, well, thrilling. Camille is on cloud nine."

"But you're not?" he asks her warily, splashing water into his Ricard to dilute it. "Oh yes, I am, Michel. You know that."

"Where have you been?"

"Rue Perrée Central Police station. With Gaston Leclerc and Camille, making statements. There was some doubt about Gaston's jurisdiction outside of Cognac until they saw the footage the director had shot in the studio. Now Gaston is the man of the moment. The press was all over the place after you snuck away."

"I see."

"And Dr. Chevanne's medical testimony will nail Fieschi and Antonelli. Tell me how you did it, Michel. Where did you get the photographs and that bloody contract my father was obviously forced to sign by Fieschi?"

"Not now, Jeanne. Now is not the time. What about us?"

She takes a good pull on her wine: "God, I could do with a cigarette." She looks away as if searching for inspiration.

"So could I, if it makes any difference."

Jeanne takes a breath: "After a year of living with Fieschi in that dreadful mausoleum on Rue Guénégaud I asked him why he is the way he is." She pauses a beat. "And don't forget, I was a poor deluded child bride." She is still looking into the distance. "And what did he say?"

"'Je suis comme je suis ... I am as I am.' I'll never forget that." She pauses again, lost in thought. "And after I stormed out of the

174

Georges V that day, I asked myself the same question in the back of the taxi."

"And?" Michel asks again, dreading the answer.

"I am as I am, Michel. Stubborn to the very last. That's the real me. I could never forgive you for deceiving me the way you did."

"But Jeanne, listen ..."

"No, no. no, you listen," she says. "If we'd stayed together after that phone call you received from Noah, I'd always be bringing it up in the future. Any time we had a row or even a simple misunderstanding, I'd remind you of the Nazi Cognac and your duplicity. I'd be impossible. I know I would."

"You're honest, I give you that." Michel says, surprised at her frankness. "Camille and I are chalk and cheese in temperament. She's compliant and agreeable. I am the opposite. It's always been that way."

"Unyielding?"

"That's the right word, yes. Camille would agree if you asked her. And I really think you should." She gives him that look.

Jeanne takes a final sip of her wine and discreetly tucks a fifty Euro note under her glass: "We will always be friends, Michel. And I'll never forget what you did for Camille and me tonight." She gets off the barstool gracefully. "It was the ultimate liberation. Now I must go. Please appreciate what I've just said. It wasn't easy."

Michel stands courteously: "I'll see you out."

"No need ... there's a taxi waiting for me."

Michel says: "Let me understand this clearly. Are you saying I should ask Camille?" Jeanne pecks him on the cheek: "Yes, that's exactly what I am saying. And I know she'd be disappointed if you didn't."

She leaves without another word. Michel sits back on his stool. Eric comes over and plucks the note from under Jeanne's half-empty glass: "You're full of surprises aren't you, Michel ... one for the road?"

Hôpital

Hôpital de la Pitié-Salpêtrière, 75013 Paris

MICHEL, JEANNE, AND CAMILLE had treated themselves to breakfast at Georges V's Galerie restaurant. That is to say, Jeanne treated them. The reason for the celebration was that she'd received a settlement cheque – on behalf of the two sisters - from Fieschi's Corsican lawyers for two million Euros. That was the estimated cost of refurbishing Château Boissier. Inspector Gaston Leclerc's team in Cognac had pressed for Fieschi's criminal conviction on a range of charges. They couldn't prove the murder of Gérard and Edith, but they could prove extortion and he'd been sentenced to ten years in prison. But the financial settlement for the twins had been a separate – an out-of-court matter – and was dealt with swiftly. Serge Antonelli was also arrested for being implicit in embezzlement and financial impropriety.

The other reason for them going to the Galerie was Michel was desperate for an American breakfast. Although he was Canadian

177

and loved un petit déjeuner, he'd had sufficient croissants, baguettes and confiture to last him a lifetime. He craved pancakes with maple syrup, bacon and toast. The two girls had watched him devour a plateful with three black coffees. They stayed traditional.

*

The three of them walk down Boulevard de L'Hôpital to keep their appointment which had been booked six weeks earlier by Michel and Camille. The sign on the door said:

DR LUC SILVANT

MAXILLO-FACIAL SURGEON

Now Michel and Jeanne sit quietly in the waiting room, admiring numerous framed accolades: medical diplomas, certificates, honorary positions in assorted university hospitals. There are also several black and white photos of war zones and an award from Médecins Sans Frontières.

*

Inside the consulting room, Camille is lying on a hospital examination couch looking at the computer screen. A gloved nurse emerges with her copious patient notes, the results of various MRI and CT scans and places them on a desk.

Dr. Silvant is a charismatic man of fifty. His pockmarked skin and rugged looks add to his compelling personality. He's dressed in theatre greens and his tunic reveals muscular forearms covered with tufts of black hair and assorted scars. He sits at a swivel chair beside the couch. He removes his silver-framed glasses and regards Camille with concern: "You've never had these scars looked at before? Other than the medics who attended you the night of the fire in Cognac?" He's studying Camille's medical notes and looking at her at the same time.

The question surprises her: "No." She hesitates, embarrassed. "My guardian said cosmetic surgery was the height of vanity and should be avoided."

Silvant huffs with annoyance: "Did he now? Then your guardian is a fool, with respect. Botox injections might be considered vain. But what we are proposing is a corrective surgical procedure. Entirely different." He pauses to form an explanation that will be helpful. "Our job here is to permanently restore areas of skin that have been affected by scarring ... this can have been caused genetically or accidently – as is true in your case. I can see from your notes ... you were rescued from a fire ...15 juin 2018 ... down in the Charente."

Camille nods: "Yes."

"Who suggested you consult me? That's more than five years ago?"

"My husband."

Silvant's face crinkles into a smile: "The good news is that we

179

can fix your scars, Camille. Burns are never simple to treat, but things have changed greatly in the years I have practised here. That's the upside of war ..." He pauses and waits for the inevitable response.

"War?"

Silvant chuckles: "Yes, all these conflicts around the world have taught us how to manage and treat burns. I have worked in the Middle East, Afghanistan, and Tunisia." He glances at the wall of evidence.

"I see, yes, I understand ... you've obviously travelled a lot with Médecins Sans Frontières?"

"Indeed, I have, yes." Silvant flexes his fingers: "Good. Anyway, your back should present no real difficulties. I am going to have a dermatologist look too. I'm going to call her right now."

He punches numbers and waits: "Eloise, it's Luc. Can you pop down, please?" Camille says: "And the bad news?"

"There is no bad news. You may need a while off work to recuperate. Does that present a problem?"

"No, I sold the confectionary shop. I've got a château to restore with my husband Michel and my sister Jeanne."

A lightbulb moment: "Confiserie Boissier, the shop on Rue du Poitou?" "That's me ... or was, yes."

"I knew I'd seen you before somewhere, but I didn't like to ask where. Not very professional. Boissier makes the best bonbons in

Paris. I take my daughter there on a Saturday. Well, well."

"Let's hope that tradition continues. There is no reason why it shouldn't." Camille settles her head back on the uncomfortable hospital pillow and thinks. She could have quite fancied Dr Luc Silvant if she wasn't already married to Michel, a man she cared for more deeply about than she could ever have imagined. And she knew Michel felt the same about her too. Life is full of surprises.

"Camille?" asks Silvant. "We can operate in three weeks. Does that work for you?" She doesn't have to look in her diary to tell him it does.

Reincarnation

Château Boissier, Segonzac, Charente

THE SURGERY WAS TRANSFORMATIVE. Everybody on Dr Luc Silvant's team was delighted. After a month's recuperation at a hotel in Gstaad, she was ready for her final follow-up appointment with Luc. She walked into his clinic at Hôpital Pitié-Salpêtrière and he was mesmerised at how fantastic she looked. It was hard for him to be dispassionate and professional. He absorbed her gentle features, golden skin, slightly freckled. A certain innocence in those arctic blue eyes. The blonde hair, slightly wavy, completed a picture of beauty. He was reminded of the paintings by Etienne Adolphe, but more significantly, the likeness to her twin sister, Jeanne. It was uncanny.

Luc and Eloise gave Camille a final examination and declared her 100% fit. As the door of the clinic closed, Luc turned to his colleague and said: "The only word I can think of is Reincarnation. That young woman has been born again and I wish her all the good fortune the world can give her."

"I agree," Eloise said to him. "Totally."

*

The château too was a transformation. It cost nearly two million Euros to restore; and two years of hard work by numerous skilled artisans. The builder from Lignières-Sonneville had been entirely accurate in his estimation of the cost and timeframe. So had an eminent local architect called Odette Chevalier. She was a dainty lady of thirty who as at home on a scaffold with workmen as she was sitting at her drawing board.

But it had been worth every centime and Jeanne and Camille were now more than happy with the result. "It's now been transformed from a burnt-out wreck into a building of local historical importance. And magnificence." That's how Odette had described it over a glass of chilled Pineau des Charentes, the night they finished. The local mayor came to cut the ribbon and declared it 'terminé.'

Had Dr Luc Silvant been present, he might have said the château too, was a Reincarnation.

*

Camille, in the first trimester of pregnancy, now walks gingerly from the kitchen door towards the rear of the château to the ramshackle barns and Cognac chais.   She opens the large old wooden door with her outstretched right hand and she's inside

183

amongst the clutter of old Cognac barrels, broken garden furniture and engine parts. It's semi dark and silent. Bright shafts of sunlight shine through the broken roof. They shimmer and dance before her illuminating tiny motes of dust. Her breaths are audible. Just ahead of her are the two child handshapes imprinted on the wall in white paint. The ones that had haunted Jeanne that fateful afternoon. Camille slowly reaches out and touches her own print with the palm of her hand. She swallows with tension.

"For posterity?" asks Michel softly, behind her.

Camille swings around, startled. Then she sees Michel's face and strokes it softly: "You surprised me ... do you know about these two – our father Gérard dipped our hands in a tray of white paint when we were little. This has always been a special place for Jeanne and me. We think sometimes he is with us ... in different ways. Supporting us. Protecting us."

Yes, Jeanne told me. The afternoon we first met ... all that time ago." Camille instinctively touches her swollen belly with a nod. It's not a memory she wishes to share. He understands. Then he takes her head in his hand and kisses her: "But your father was right, you know, Camille."

She pulls away, confused. He looks her in the eyes and touches her belly. "What was my father right about?"

"For future generations ... You two are my angels now."

His words evoke in her a special significance as she places her palm on her childhood handprint once more. She hasn't told him yet that she's expecting twins.

*

Michel and Camille wander down to the newly landscaped garden from the Cognac chais to a table where Michel had been sitting earlier. Aunt Bénédicte appears to be asleep in a deck chair, a curious wicker basket by her side.

Jeanne sifts through numerous papers on the table to make some space for the decanter of orange squash and glasses she's brought. She stumbles upon Michel's crumpled German maps and papers from 1940. "I thought you'd got rid of all this Noah Gagnon paraphernalia, Michel?"

"I thought I had." He glances at Camille, who looks away, irritated. "Clearly not. They're right here amongst this bundle of architect's drawings and builders' quotes." As if to say bona fide château documents, not papers from the Canadian who'd inadvertently caused them so much grief.

Michel shakes his head: "Sorry, Jeanne. I really thought I'd binned them. Does it really matter? It's history now."

Jeanne folds the maps and looks at him: "Yes, I know. But don't you still think it was a long shot to expect to find Cognac that vanished after the war?" She still must make a point even though the matter was closed the day she stormed out of the Georges V suite. Michel shoots Camille a look: "Yes, of course you are right, Jeanne ... come and sit down here, Camille."

185

She sits on his lap, heavily. He groans with a smile: "What a lump."

"Well! There are two of us here! Maybe even three."

"What did you just say? Three?" He looks bemused but she smiles as if to say – nothing, my dear, you'll find out in time.

Presently, Pascal, Marie-Christine and their children appear from the vineyards breathless. Pascal is panting with exertion: "Have we covered some distance! Whoa! I feel as if we walked a thousand kilometres! Thirsty work! I need a drink ..." He pours himself squash from the decanter filled with juice and ice. "I need this!"

Jeanne turns to her sister: "Are you alright, Camille?"

Camille nods, but no she is not. She's sick of her sister still raking up the past. Pascal sinks his squash: "Michel, have you got a proper drink? This stuff is for kids!" Aunt Bénédicte suddenly stirs: "I've got something that might be of more interest than squash." From her basket she pulls out a dusty old bottle; the label is ancient.

COGNAC MASSOUGNES VINTAGE 1805

Michel, Jeanne and Camille look at one another dumbfounded.

Pascal finishes his squash and regards the label with interest: "1805 was the year of the Battle of Trafalgar. English victory over the French and Spanish by the Royal Navy." Jeanne asks: "Where did this come from, Aunt Bénédicte?"

Bénédicte smiles: "Did you ever meet Louis Doupeux?"

"No," Jeanne replies bluntly.

"There is no reason why you should have, I suppose. We were in love, years ago." The girls are mystified: they know nothing of Bénédicte's past in Paris. She puts the Massougnes back in her basket, and looks dreamily into the distance, remembering. "Louis owned an old hotel, La Vie en Rose in Paris. The restaurant dated back to 1582, supposedly. They had a terrible flood and discovered a thousand bottles of an 1875 Armagnac, hidden in a secret cellar. Louis sold them at a Sotheby's auction in London. It brought enough money for him to retire to La Rochelle; a very spacious flat overlooking the harbour."

"And?" Jeanne wants her to get on with the story.

"Louis passed away last year; I went to the funeral. His widow Agathe told me he'd left something for me in the garage. An old crate from the restaurant. I had to hire a removal company to bring it back here."

"What was in it?" This time it is Camille who is interested.

"I'll show you." She reaches into her basket and retrieves a list which she hands to Michel to read out aloud.

He clears his throat with mounting disbelief:

"1805 LA PLUS ANCIENNE – 1811 ROIS DE ROME – 1834 PRINCE ALBERT – 1840 LOUIS PHILIPPE – 1858 NAPOLEON 111 EMPEREUR ..."

Bénédicte interrupts: "I drank that last Christmas ... hazelnuts I seem to recall. Carry on, Michel."

He continues: "1875 PRINCE IMPERIAL – 1889 EXCELLENCE and, finally, 1893 AGE D'OR. This is extraordinary, Bénédicte. Wait, there are some notes." He pauses and reads on – then, having understood the words, carries on reading aloud:

"After decades of ageing in oaken casks, these venerable Cognacs have been transferred to wax-sealed demijohns, where they are preserved intact. Natural evaporation – known as – the Angels' Share – has reduced the alcoholic strength of the oldest of them to as little as 30%, leaving only the quintessence of the finest scents of Cognac. Despite their age, they have retained their vigour and personality and deserve to be tasted just as they are. Don't mention this gift to the French Government. Agathe would have to sell her soul to pay the Duty. I'll love you always, Bénédicte. I married the wrong woman. Louis xxx"

"There we are then, girls. The cat is out of the bag," says Bénédicte with a mischievous smile.

"A whole litter of them," says Michel, trying to lighten the impact of the incredible revelation.

Bénédicte looks at him: "You noticed the empty NAPOLEON

bottle when you came over that day, didn't you, Michel. It was on the shelf. I thought you were going to ask me questions about it."

Michel recalls the exact moment: "Yes, other questions took precedence." Camille says: "Where are they now?"

"Chez moi." At home, she says proudly.

"What are you going to do with them? Sell them?" asks Jeanne, with an edge she cannot disguise.

Bénédicte narrows her eyes: "I'd have to see the colour of your money, first young lady." The old lady's expression melts into a wicked smile. She can read Jeanne like a book. Jeanne gasps in embarrassment: "Oh, Aunt Bénédicte, I didn't mean anything like that. Honestly, I didn't!"

"I know you didn't, dear. They are for you two. A gift from me to you … For future generations, my two angels … Isn't that what your Papa Gérard used to say?"

THE END

Thank You:

Especially to my wife Pam for her love and patience; and to Marianne, always my first and trusted reader.

To J.P. for such a great edit and for providing so many creative suggestions throughout the lengthy process.

To Len Greenwood, my publisher at TradShack. Thank you for all the great artwork and continued enthusiasm for my work.

To David Baker at Hermitage Cognac who inspired many ideas about old Cognac!

A Note from the Author

After an excellent Dégustation at Aux Délices du Terroir in Criteuil-la-Magdeleine in the heart of the Charente, I returned to my chambre d'hôte. I lay on a sun lounger by the pool and fell into a deep sleep. The dream I had was vivid:

In the gardens of a burned-out château a man (Michel) meets a woman called Jeanne. He's a dashing French-Canadian looking at properties and she is a beautiful French girl. This is the place where she grew up with her sister Camille. She's there to commemorate the anniversary of their parents who were killed in the fire. Camille is unable to attend.

Michel and Jeanne have a brief flirtation, but the romance goes no further because she is married, although unhappily. In the morning, he discovers she has vanished from the Hostellerie where they are both staying. He must find her.

I was certain this idea would work as a story.

*

On 17th May 2013, I found a discarded copy of Le Monde on the TGV from Angoulême to Paris. On the front page was a picture of a young actress – Marine Vacth – and the headline:

CANNES UNE ÉTOILE BRILLE AU PREMIER JOUR

It occurred to me that what if our French-Canadian, Michel, meets a celebrated film star in the gardens of the château, but doesn't recognise her? Then Michel finds a discarded copy of the newspaper on the TGV. And he must find her.

This premise I developed into a French screenplay first called LA PART DES ANGES (The Angels' Share) which I still believe would make a fabulous film and could be made in the Poitou-Charentes and Paris.

Robert Wallace - October 2023

IV

ROBERT WALLACE

VALENTINES CUP

The first story in the Valentine Series

1943 Bavaria

Undercover agent Alistair Valentine
overhears a few words that will
alter the course of the war

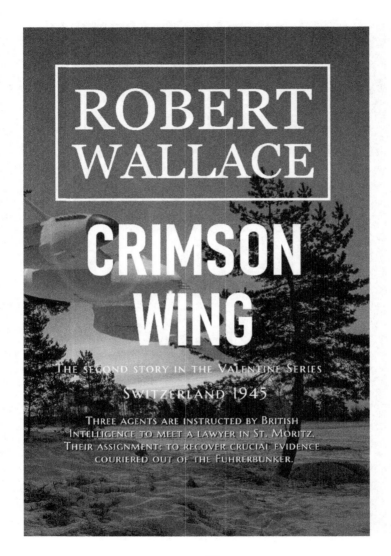

ROBERT WALLACE

CRIMSON WING

THE SECOND STORY IN THE VALENTINE SERIES

SWITZERLAND 1945

THREE AGENTS ARE INSTRUCTED BY BRITISH
INTELLIGENCE TO MEET A LAWYER IN ST. MORITZ.
THEIR ASSIGNMENT: TO RECOVER CRUCIAL EVIDENCE
COURIERED OUT OF THE FUHRERBUNKER.

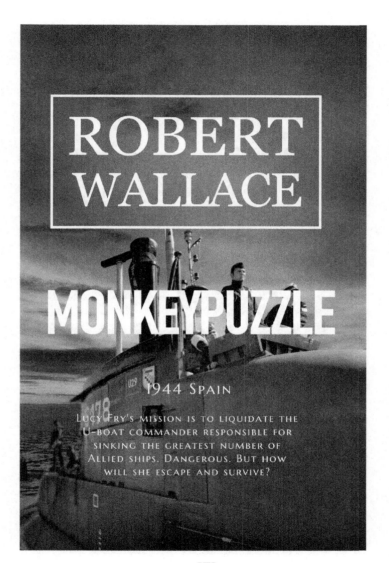

ROBERT
WALLACE

MONKEYPUZZLE

1944 Spain

Lucy Fry's mission is to liquidate the
U-boat commander responsible for
sinking the greatest number of
Allied ships. Dangerous. But how
will she escape and survive?

ROBERT WALLACE

OPERATION GUNFLEET

The final story in the Valentine Series

London 1946

Vital communications equipment has
been stolen from Bletchley Park.
Brimblecombe's team is reunited for one
final mission: recover the equipment, and
identify the traitor at the White House.

VIII

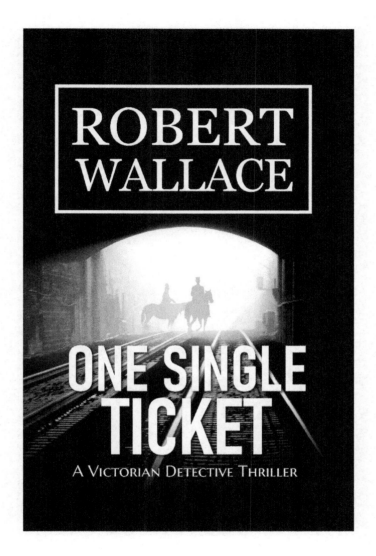

ROBERT WALLACE

ONE SINGLE TICKET

A VICTORIAN DETECTIVE THRILLER

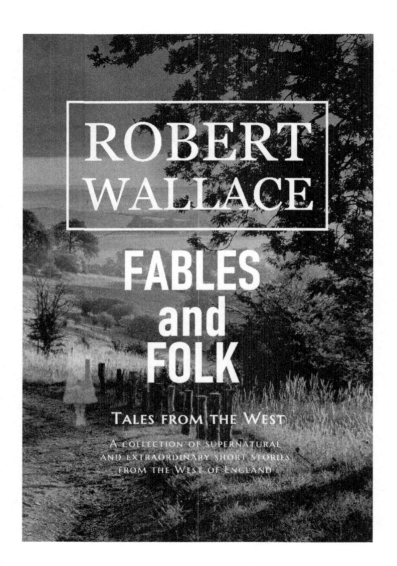

ROBERT WALLACE

FABLES and FOLK

TALES FROM THE WEST

A COLLECTION OF SUPERNATURAL
AND EXTRAORDINARY SHORT STORIES
FROM THE WEST OF ENGLAND

ROBERT WALLACE

THE BETRAYAL OF JACQUELINE FLOWER

A PSYCHOLOGICAL CRIME THRILLER WITH
AN INTRICATE AND TWISTING STORYLINE

XI

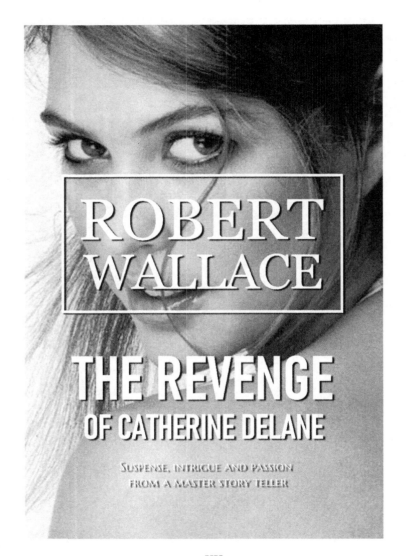

ROBERT
WALLACE

THE REVENGE
OF CATHERINE DELANE

SUSPENSE, INTRIGUE AND PASSION
FROM A MASTER STORY TELLER

XIII

Printed in Great Britain
by Amazon